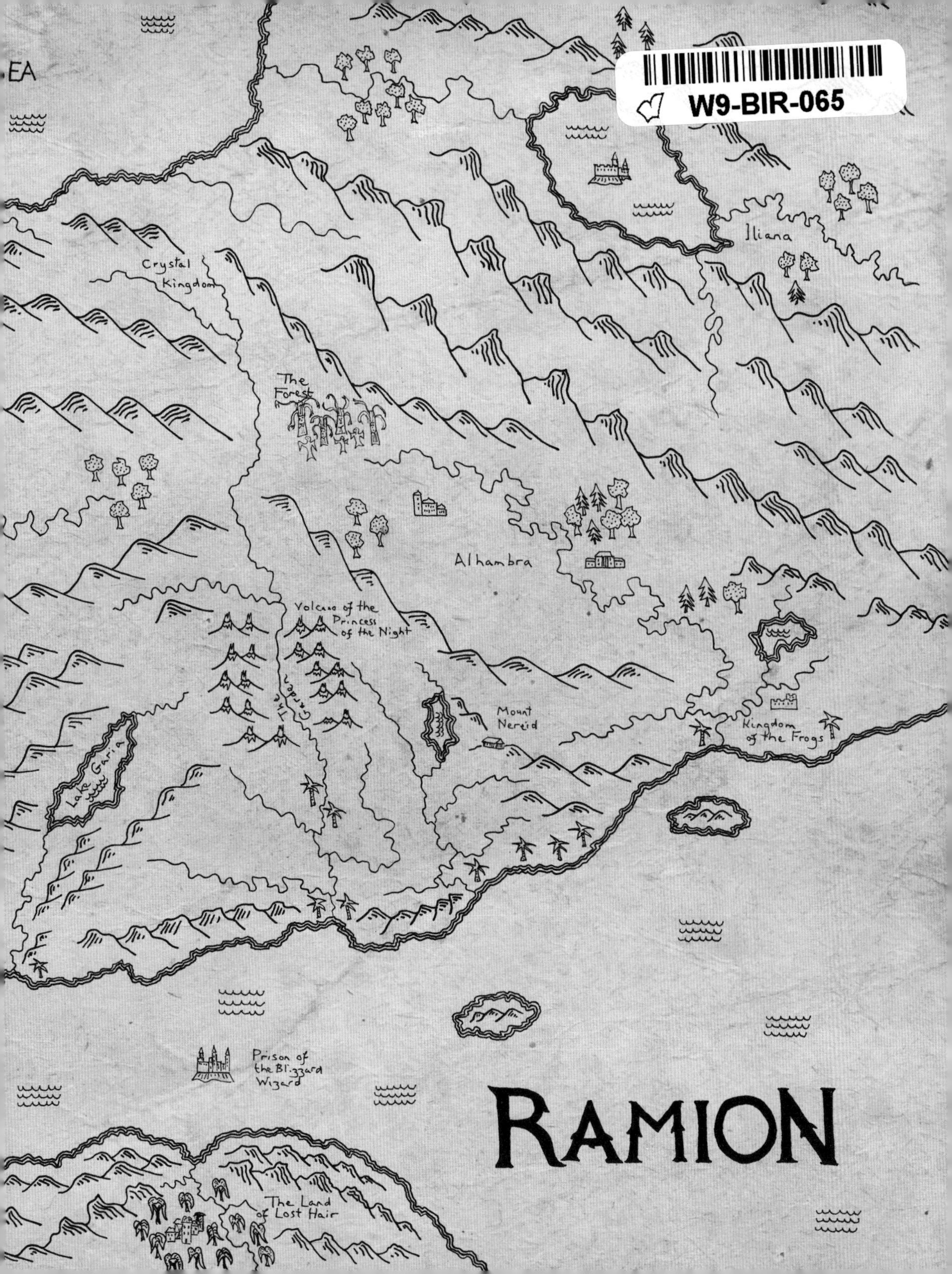
EA
Crystal Kingdom
Iliana
The Forest
Alhambra
Volcano of the Princess of the Night
The Garden
Mount Nereid
Kingdom of the Frogs
Lake Garia
Prison of the Blizzard Wizard
The Land of Lost Hair
RAMION

THE
GIFT OF EVIL

Published by

Perronet Press

www.ramion-books.com

Copyright © Text and illustrations

Frank Hinks 2019

The author has asserted his moral rights
A CIP record for this book is available from the British Library

ISBN: 9781909938298

Printed in China by CP Printing Ltd.
Layout by Jennifer Stephens
Font designer - Bajo La Luna Producciones

TALES of RAMION

THE GIFT OF EVIL

FRANK HINKS

Perronet

2019

TALES OF RAMION

THE GARDENER

Lord of Ramion, guardian and protector

THE GUIDE

Friend and servant of the Gardener

SNUGGLE

Dream Lord sent to protect the boys from the witch Griselda

THE MIDWIFE

Comes in the name of the Gardener

GRISELDA A CHILD

Aspires to be a witch
(the traditional kind)

BORIS AUSTIN

Griselda's best friend
(until turned into a floating skull)

GRISELDA'S DAD

A Grunch but good!

THE PRINCESS OF
THE NIGHT

Lord of Nothingness, source of evil

GARESHA

Witch of the Order of the Night

SERVANTS OF
THE NIGHT

*Of swirling shades of
black and grey*

ALBEE THE ALBATROSS

Spy of the Princess, harbinger of doom

SIR TANCRED GRUNCH

Griselda's grandpa, not nice at all

LADY GRUNCH

Of evil birth, but French

GNARGS

Warrior servants of the Princess

CHAPTER ONE

In a small vault deep beneath the ruins of Grunch Castle Griselda's dead grandfather Sir Tancred Grunch stood in a glass tank, body preserved in special fluid. Evil spirit bubbled up from his head and passing through long tubes joined evil spirit from other members of the family, was distilled in acid, and collected in bottles of darkest green. It made a lovely drink (if you are evil and like that sort of thing).

The small vault was at a distance from the vault where the bodies of other members of the family were preserved. Sir Tancred had never liked anyone very much, and in death was determined to keep well away from the bodies of his elder son David and his wife Eveline. Lady Grunch (Eveline D'Agur before she married) had never been happy with Sir Tancred sending their younger son Peter (the white sheep of the family) to Australia for doing good. What he did to David was even worse.

Sir Tancred's dead eyes were glazed and cloudy, but as with other members of the Grunch Family to be dead was not to be completely dead: there was always a chance of coming back to life, breaking out of the glass tank and making trouble. As evil spirit bubbled out of his brain Sir Tancred was deep in thought about his life.

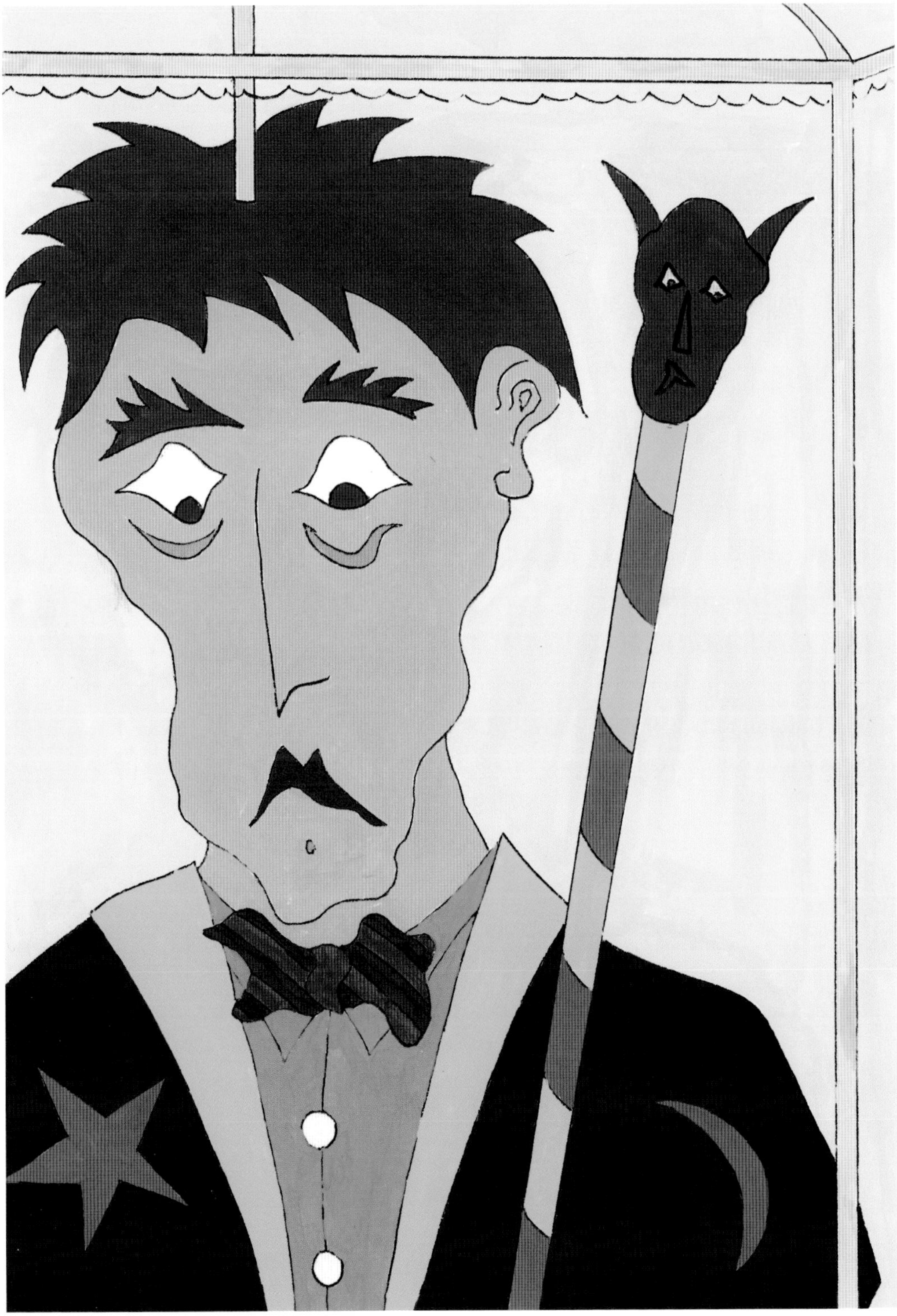

Sir Tancred regretted the evil he had failed to do (not that there had been any want of trying), but most of all he regretted that he had had two sons who had turned out to be good. The fault was not his own (or so he thought). He was a Grunch, a Grunch of Grunch Castle, a man of a truly evil family. He could say with pride that there was not a single good gene in his entire body, that he had never had a good thought or done a good deed in his entire life. Yet somehow his sons had turned out good. It was a mystery.

For long generations the Grunches had married evil women of evil birth, daughters of the D'Eaths of Fang Manor, the D'Estranges of Grisly Grange, the Bloods of Headless Hall and other families in Debrett's Evil Families of Britain. There was not a single good woman amongst them.

Sir Tancred snorted (not easy with preserving liquid up his nose). The fault must have been his wife's. The D'Agurs were an evil family, but French. One of Eveline's ancestors must have got carried away (ooh la la!) and blinded by a woman's beauty married her even though she was not of evil family.

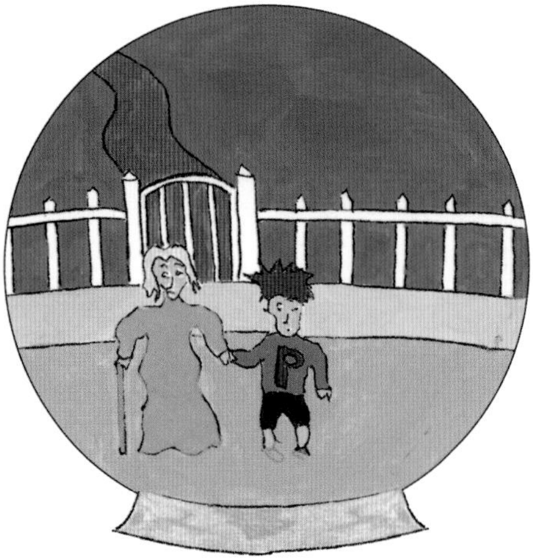
P

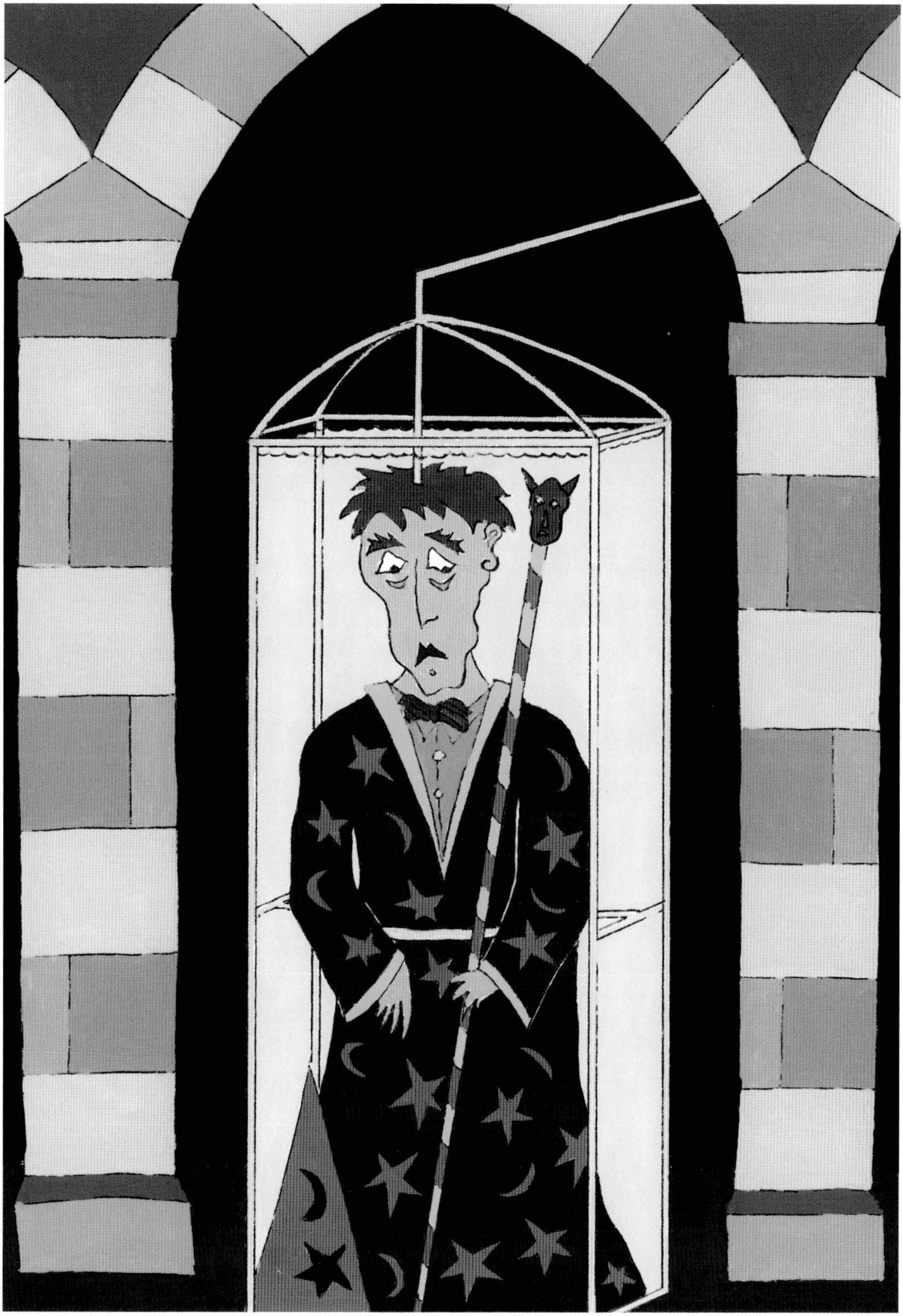

His wife Eveline always claimed this was not true, that just because she was French did not mean she was not evil through and through. Such had been their nightly quarrel each claiming to be more purely evil than the other.

The problem was their sons. To begin with both seemed quite normal. They tore the wings off bats. They cut worms in two. They dug concealed holes in the forest, traps for passing ramblers. But then one dreadful day Sir Tancred looked into his crystal ball and discovered Peter at the age of seven helping an old lady to cross the road without leaving her in the middle. It was true that Peter was only young, but that was no excuse for doing good.

Sir Tancred ranted, raved and gave Peter a choice: either he reformed and started doing evil or he would be sent to Australia. Peter did not reform and was sent to Australia where (when he grew up) he founded a Home for Ancient Poms. But what David did was even worse (or so his father thought).

When Peter was discovered doing good David affected horror. At the time Sir Tancred thought that (as was only proper) David was horrified at Peter doing good. Later he realized that David's horror was not repulsion at Peter doing good, but the fear that he too might have good lurking inside him and be sent to Australia like his brother.

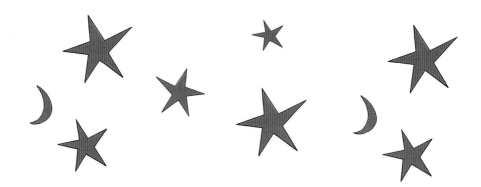

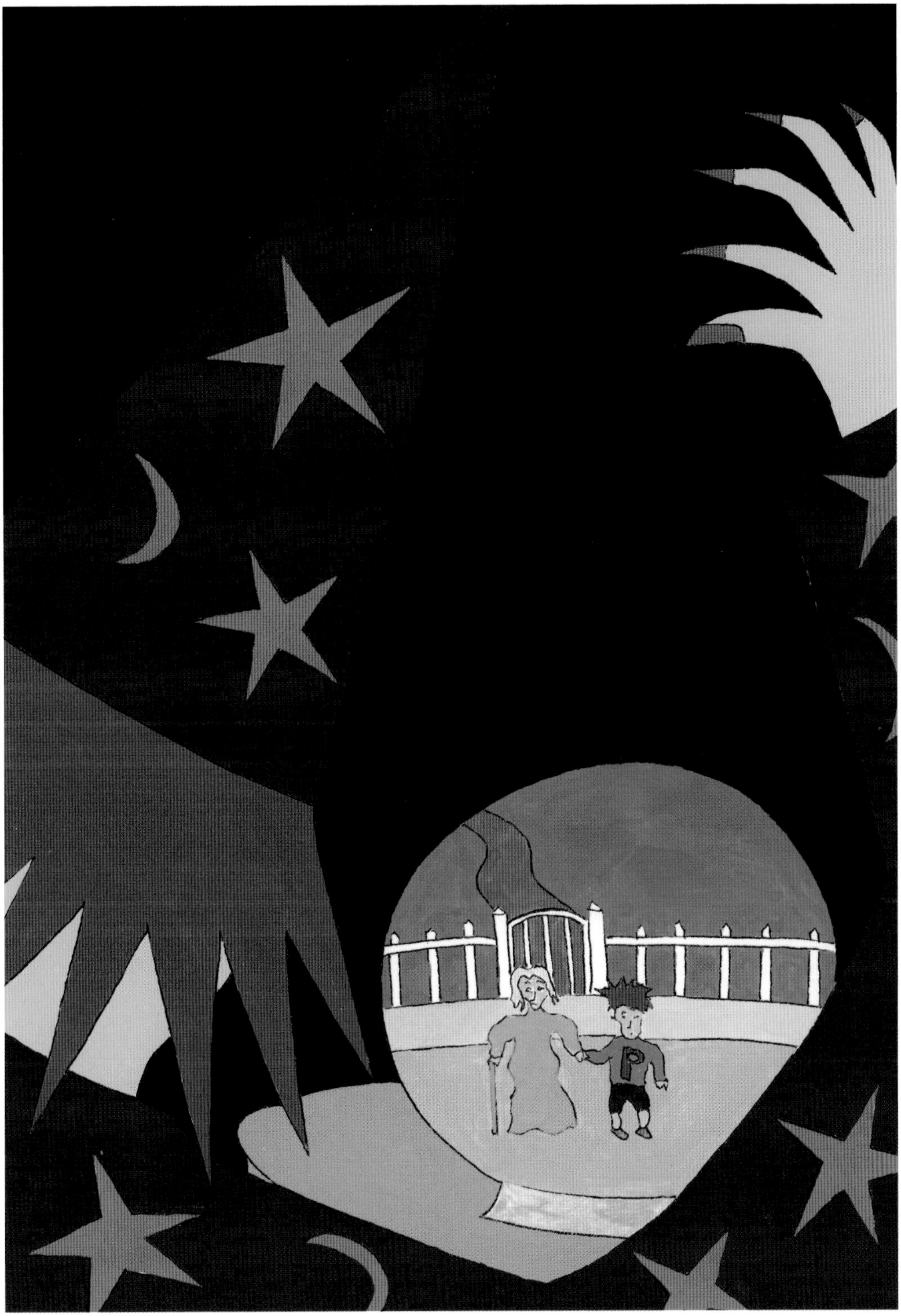

David kept a careful eye upon his thoughts and actions, fearful that they might be good. He did his best to help his father with evil spells and evil plans, but realised that he did not enjoy hurting people, that he really would prefer to do good.

David kept these dreadful thoughts well hidden until in his late teens he made the mistake of falling in love with a woman not of evil family and asking her to marry him. His choice of bride could not have been worse. Melanie was a descendant of the Wise Woman of Shoreham whose white magic had from generation to generation kept the villagers safe from the Grunches of Grunch Castle.

"When my father finds out about our engagement there will be no limit to his fury," said David to Melanie.

"What should we do?"

"Flee far from Grunch Castle."

David and Melanie married in secret and fled, but not very far. They set up home in a little semi-detached house in the suburbs of Bromley.

"The houses all look alike. My father will never find us here."

But both knew this was not so and it was not long before Sir Tancred (looking into his crystal ball) discovered their little house.

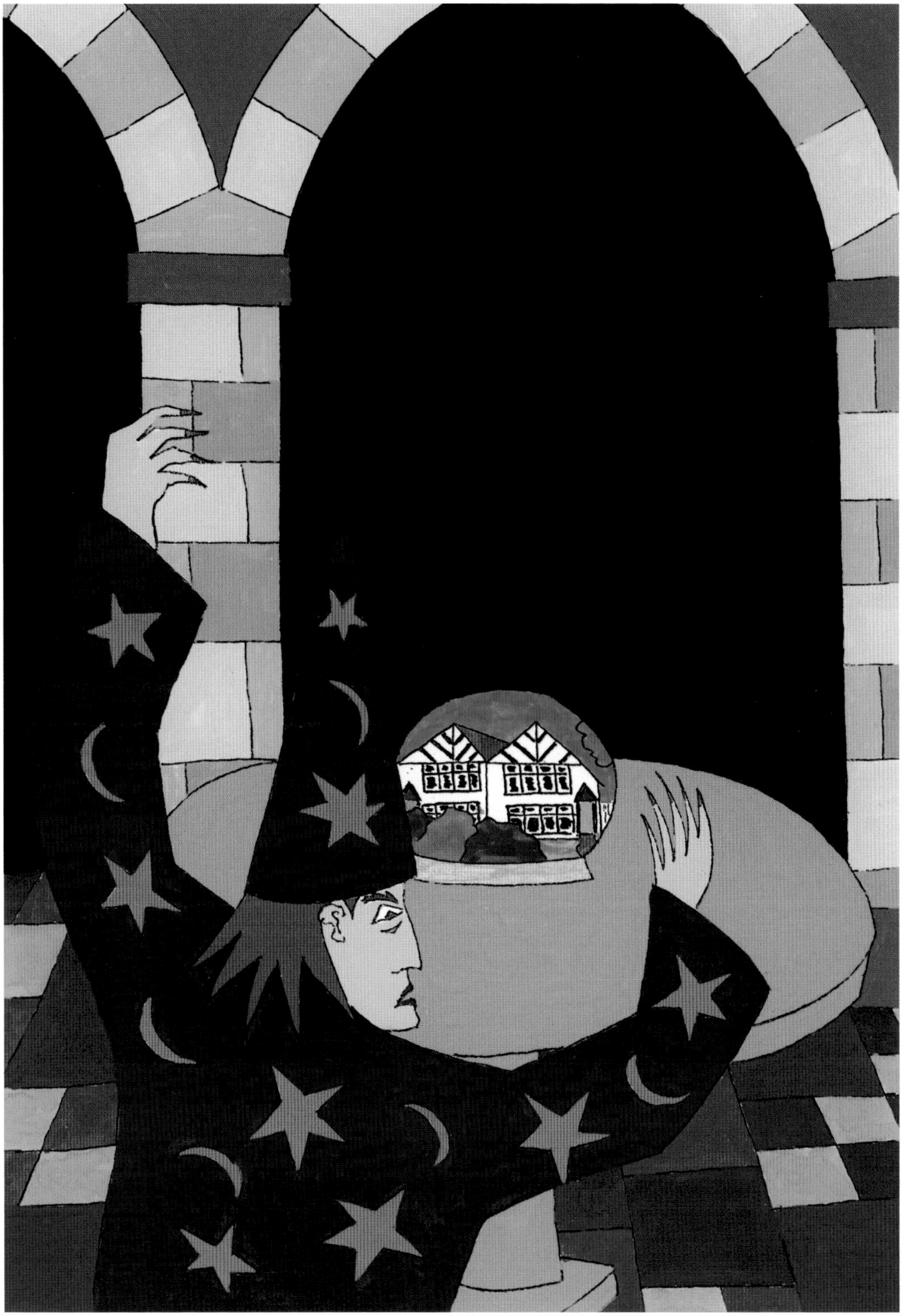

When Sir Tancred discovered David and Melanie living in their little house he ranted and raved, screamed and shouted and sent thunderbolts from his magic staff, which bounced around the remains of Grunch Castle frightening his hunchback manservant Geric.

"I will be avenged! A Grunch doing good. It is an abomination."

"You will not!" yelled his wife. "You have already sent Peter to Australia. If you send David as well I will never see my grandchildren." At this she dabbed tears from her eyes, for although of evil family she was fond of children: unlike a Grunch of Grunch Castle she had no desire to eat them. "You must promise not to send him to Australia."

"I promise," replied Sir Tancred: he had different plans for David.

"And promise nothing worse."

"I promise," hissed Sir Tancred keeping his fingers crossed behind his back so the promise would not count. He would bide his time. He would watch David and Melanie with the help of his crystal ball. They would not escape.

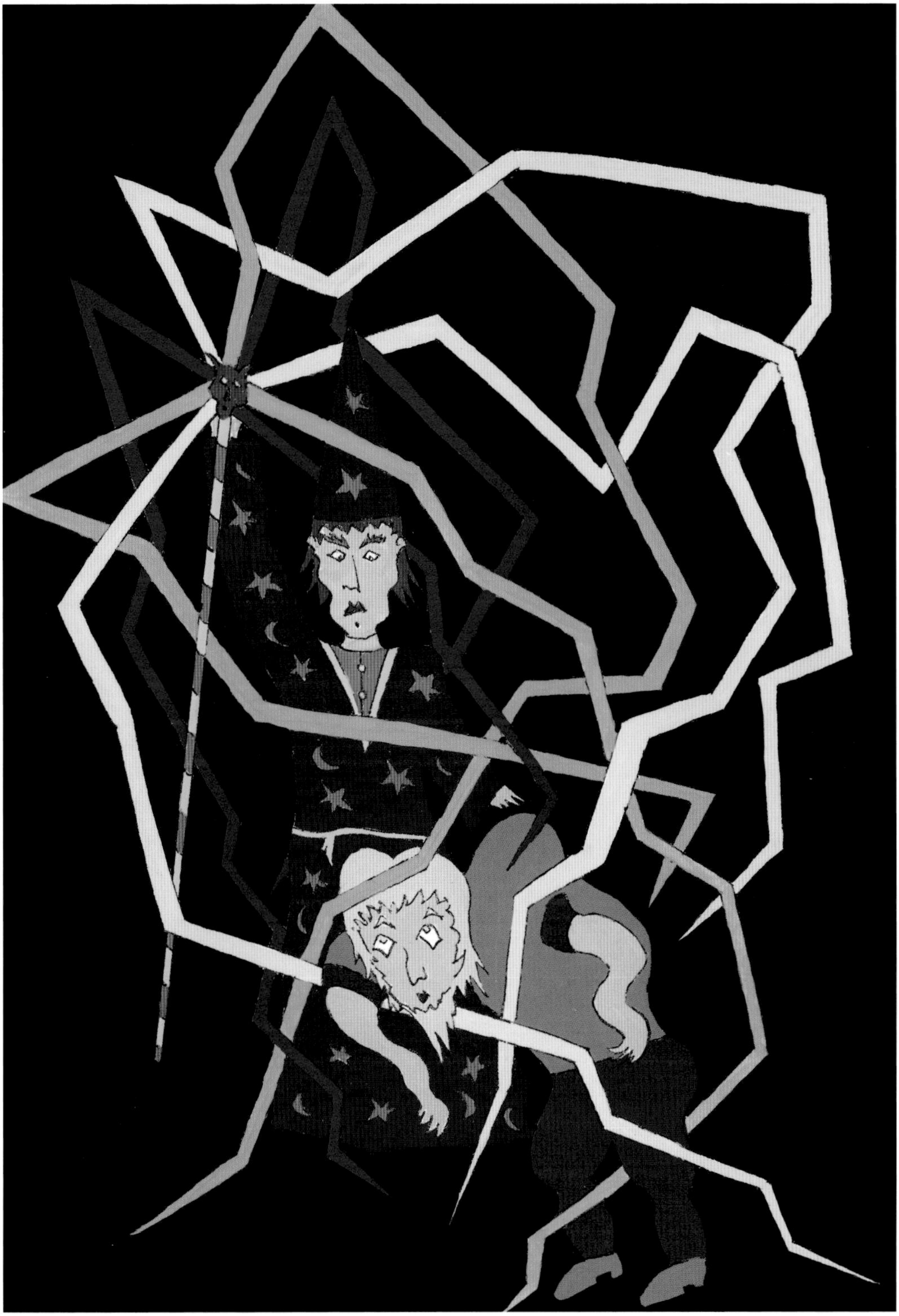

CHAPTER TWO

David and Melanie liked their little house. They decorated it in bright colours, planted flowers in the garden and kept guinea pigs which scurried around the sunken lawn. David got a job, changed out of his normal bright clothes into a suit and commuted up to London in a train. Melanie stayed at home expecting their first child. They should have been happy, but were so afraid of the child's future. What would happen to the child when Sir Tancred came to get them?

It was the day of the birth. David and Melanie were getting ready to go to hospital when there was a knock upon the front door. David opened the door. A woman was standing on the doorstep. "What do you want?" he asked.

"Take me to your wife. I am the midwife."

"But the child is to be born in hospital, not at home." David was deeply suspicious. Was this a trick of his father's? "How do I know you are who you say you are?"

"Let me talk to Melanie. Let her decide whether I am to be trusted."

Melanie (who had been hiding just inside the entrance) came forward, and looking directly at the woman asked, "Who are you?"

"My name would mean nothing. I have been sent by your ancestor, the Wise Woman of Shoreham."

"That cannot be. The Wise Woman (like my mother) is long dead."

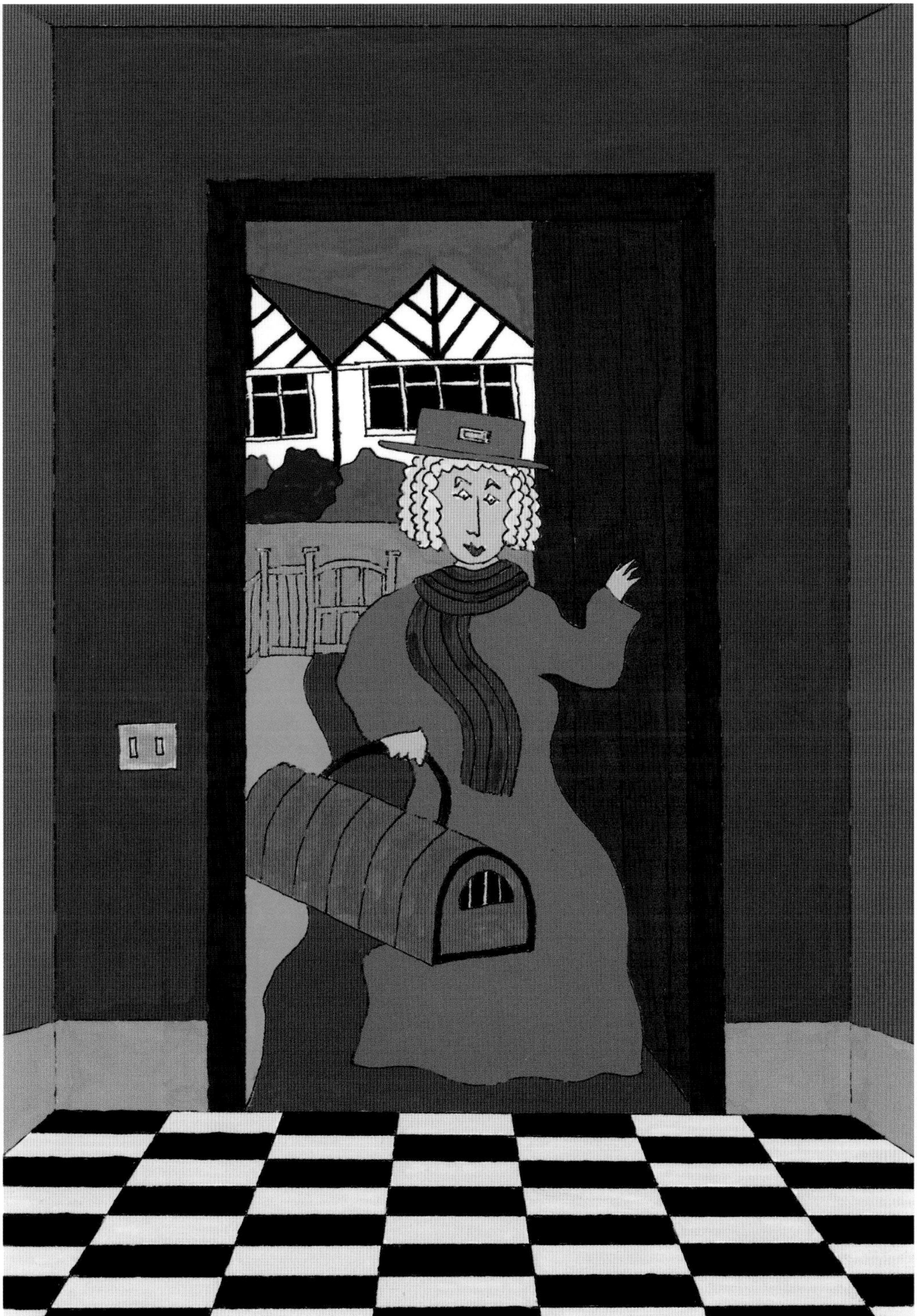

"It is not for me to explain that mystery, but let me whisper in your ear the secret name you were given at birth."

At this the little woman stretched up on tiptoe and whispered in Melanie's ear. Immediately Melanie smiled and laughed. She had not heard that name since she was tiny. "Come in! Come in! David get out of the way. Welcome our guest."

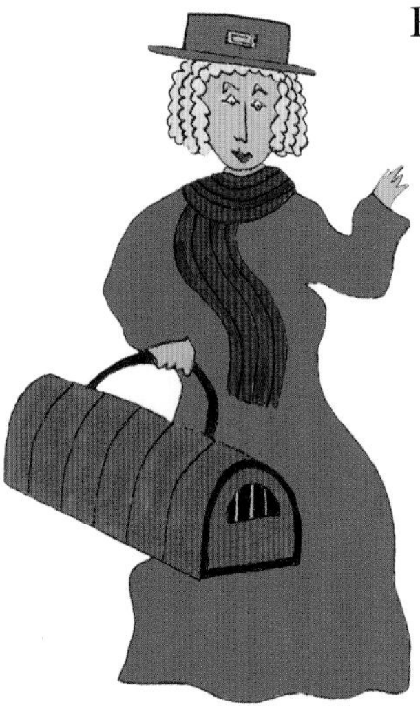

Reluctantly David moved to one side. The woman hurried in talking with great urgency. "Sir Tancred has been watching your every move. At this moment white magic blocks his vision, but it cannot hold for long – not for more than an hour at most. Sir Tancred knows you are with child. He intends to take that child: precisely when I do not know. What he does not know is that you are expecting two children, not one."

"Twins!" exclaimed Melanie.

"You must be wrong," barked David. "No one at the hospital told us that we were having twins. How could twins have been kept concealed from the doctors?"

"Another mystery my dear. A mystery it is not for me to explain. Just trust and do as I say."

"Trust! This is nonsense! How dare you come into our house and start talking rubbish," shouted David.

At this Melanie lightly brushed her husband's arm. "Hush my dear. Let her talk."

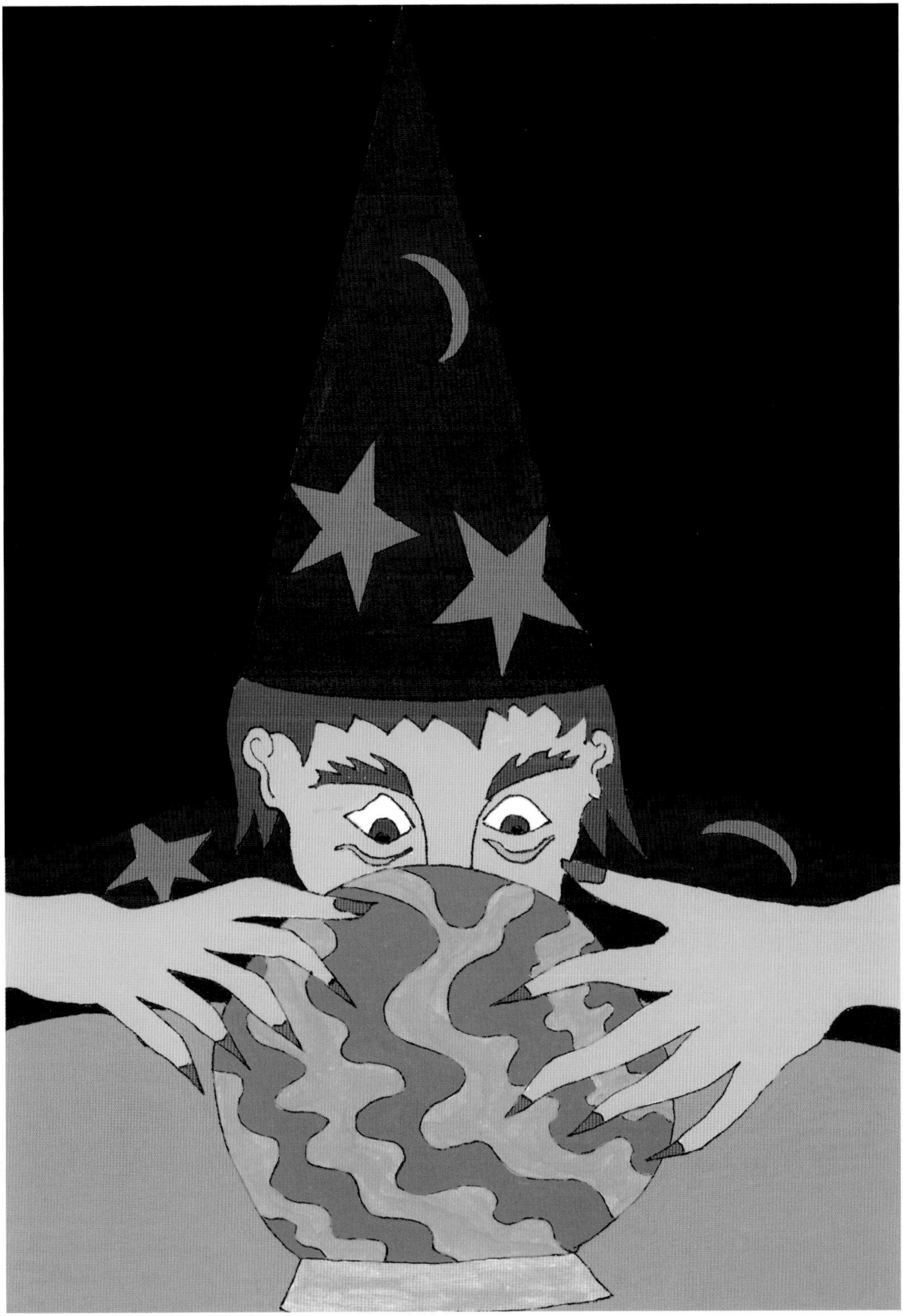

"You are about to have two daughters. Both will be descendants of the Wise Woman and the Grunches of Grunch Castle. Both will have good and evil genes. In the end each will have the choice whether to follow good or evil: it is not predetermined. But much is at stake, not just for you and your descendants. We must increase the chances of at least one child embracing the path of good. We cannot allow both to be taken by Sir Tancred."

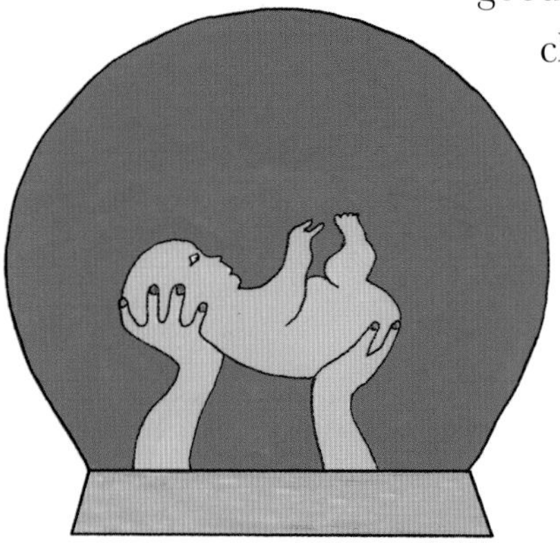

"How can we avoid that?" demanded David. "My father has great powers. He cannot easily be defeated."

"Let me speak and you will find out," observed the woman hurrying on. "You are about to have identical twins. The younger child will be called Susan: she will share the first name of the Wise Woman. You will put her up for adoption. I have the papers here." She took some legal papers out of her bag and held them out with a pen.

At this David exploded. "You're insane! You come here a complete stranger telling us we are about to have twins, that we are to sign adoption papers for the younger child, that we are to deliver her up into your hands. You are completely mad."

At this Melanie took David by the arm and said firmly, "She is not. What she whispered in my ear was not just the secret name given to me at birth, but the name of the person from whom the Wise Woman derived her powers. It is ours to listen, to trust and do what she says."

"Trust! But this is madness!"

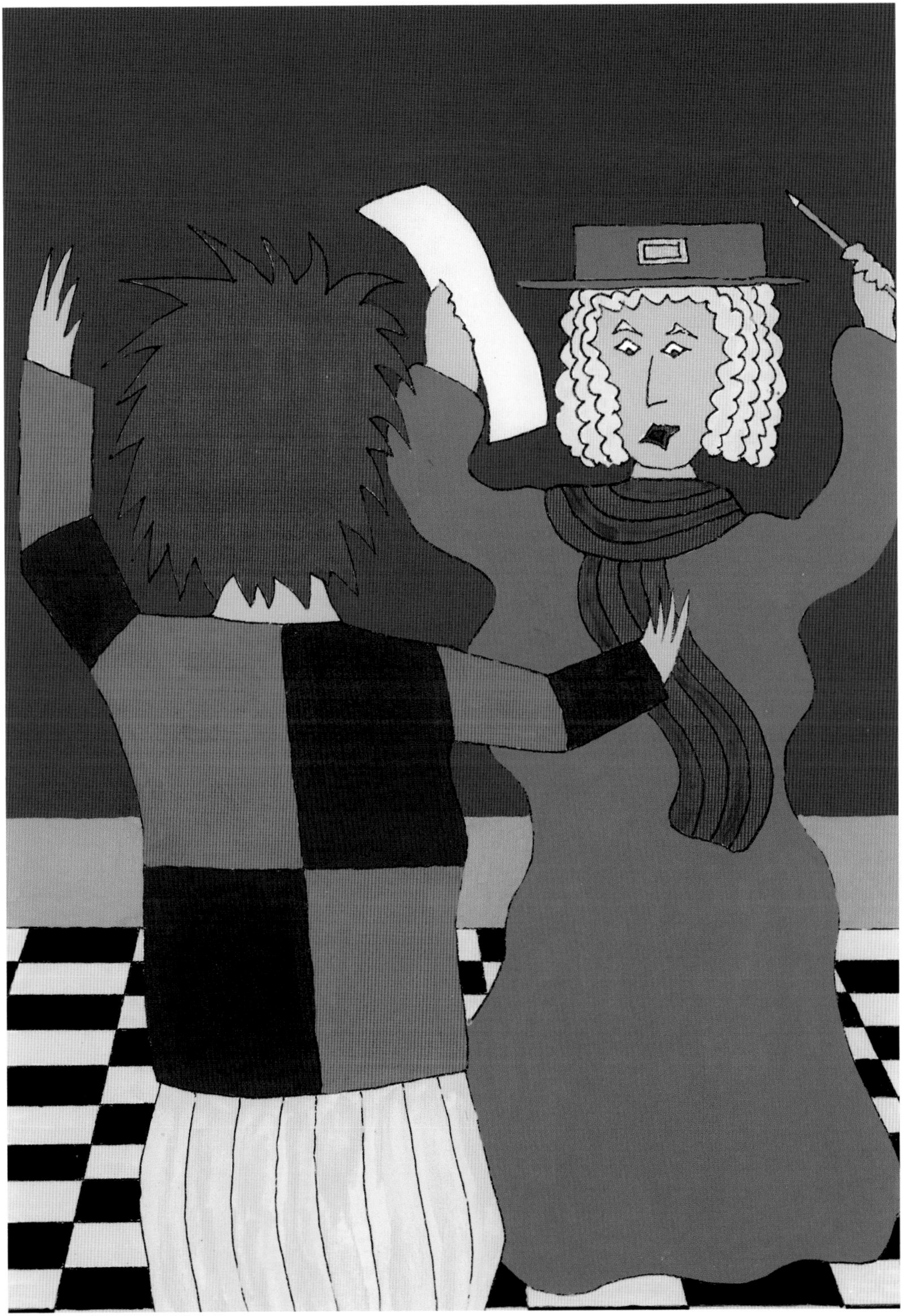

"I know it is hard for a Grunch to trust, but we must do whatever this woman tells us." Melanie signed the adoption papers. "Now you." David fell silent and without protest signed: he had never known his wife so firm, so determined. "Good woman please continue. You will take away little Susan for adoption. You will save her. But what of our elder daughter? I am frightened for her. I am frightened for her future."

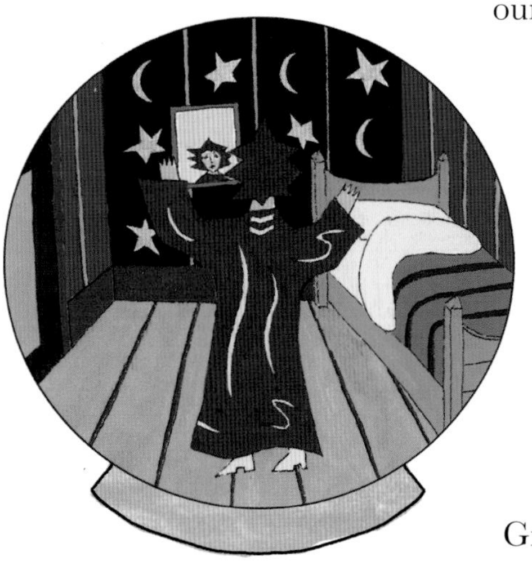

"Your elder daughter has a harder fate than that of Susan, a fate from which we cannot save her. Sir Tancred knows you are with child. He is determined to get that child. He wants an heir. We do not have the power to stop him. Your elder daughter will be called Griselda. A name used by the Grunches of Grunch Castle."

"A traditional name for a witch!"

"But not just for witches. She will be taken by Sir Tancred. Her path will be hard, far harder than that of her twin Susan, but she will have a choice, a choice between the path of good and the path of evil. Beyond that I cannot see."

"Poor little Griselda," moaned Melanie as with a gasp she grasped her belly. "My waters have broken. I am about to give birth."

Melanie gave birth to twin girls. The elder was placed in a cot beside her mother. The younger was concealed in a leather briefcase which the woman carried off.

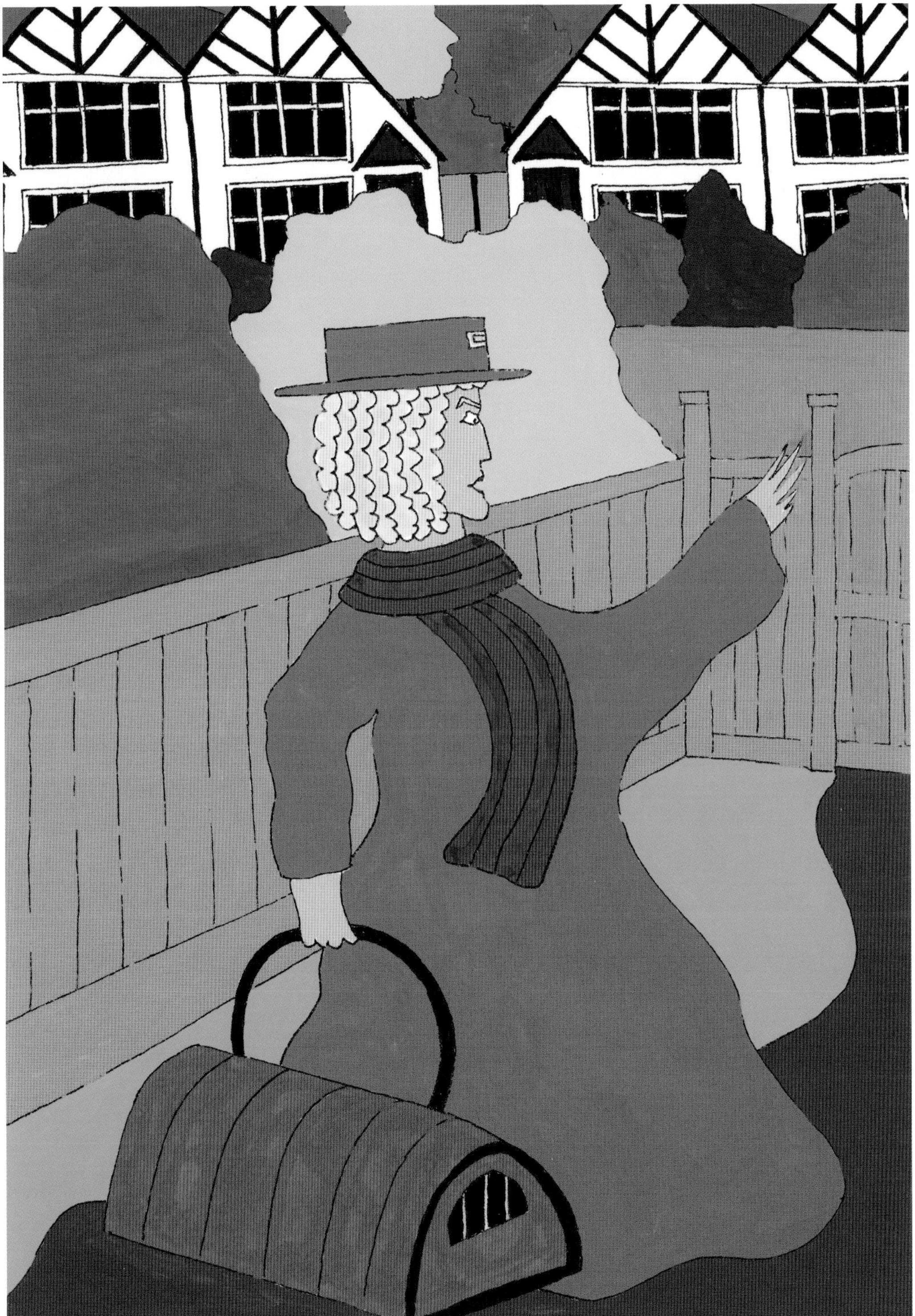

Sir Tancred had had a frustrating morning. "Bloody crystal ball!" he bellowed. "Goes on the blink! Just when it is most wanted!"

Then the vision cleared. Sir Tancred saw a tiny baby being held aloft and then placed in a cot beside Melanie. "I've missed the birth! What is the baby's name?" He adjusted the crystal ball and listened carefully.

"Griselda! An excellent name. Griselda the Grunch, Hereditary Keeper of Grunch Castle. An heir!"

Sir Tancred paused for thought.

"Grunch Castle needs an heir, but I do not want a mewling baby. I shall wait until her fifth birthday. Then I shall take her."

When Albee the Albatross (spy of the Princess of the Night) reported to his mistress that Sir Tancred was leaving Griselda with her parents until the age of five she hissed and seethed and bellowed with anger.

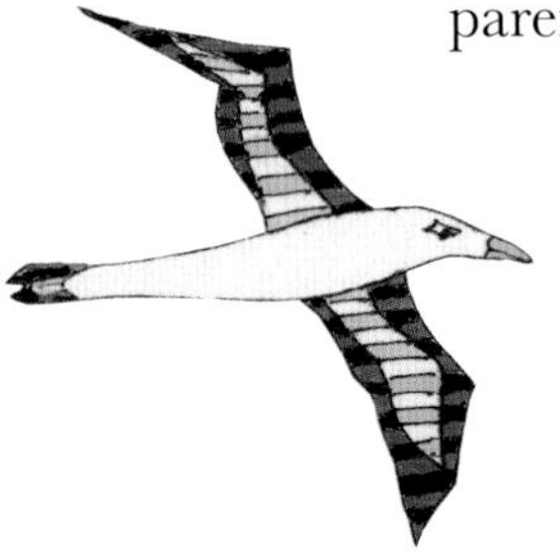

"Stupid man! By the age of five Griselda may be set in the path of good, not the path of evil. We must take no chances. I shall send her birthday presents." So saying the Princess summoned one of her witches. "Garesha! This is a job for you."

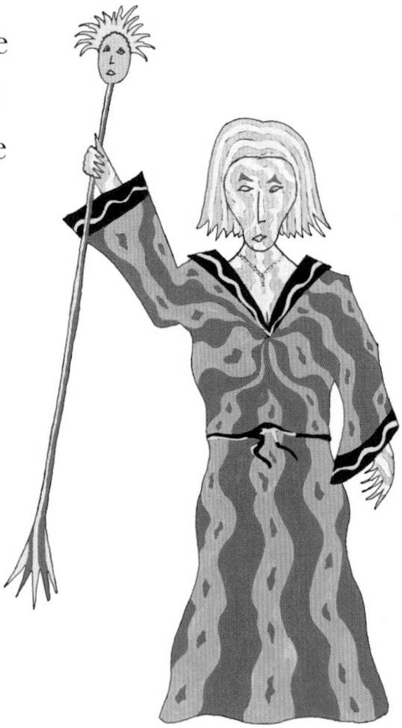

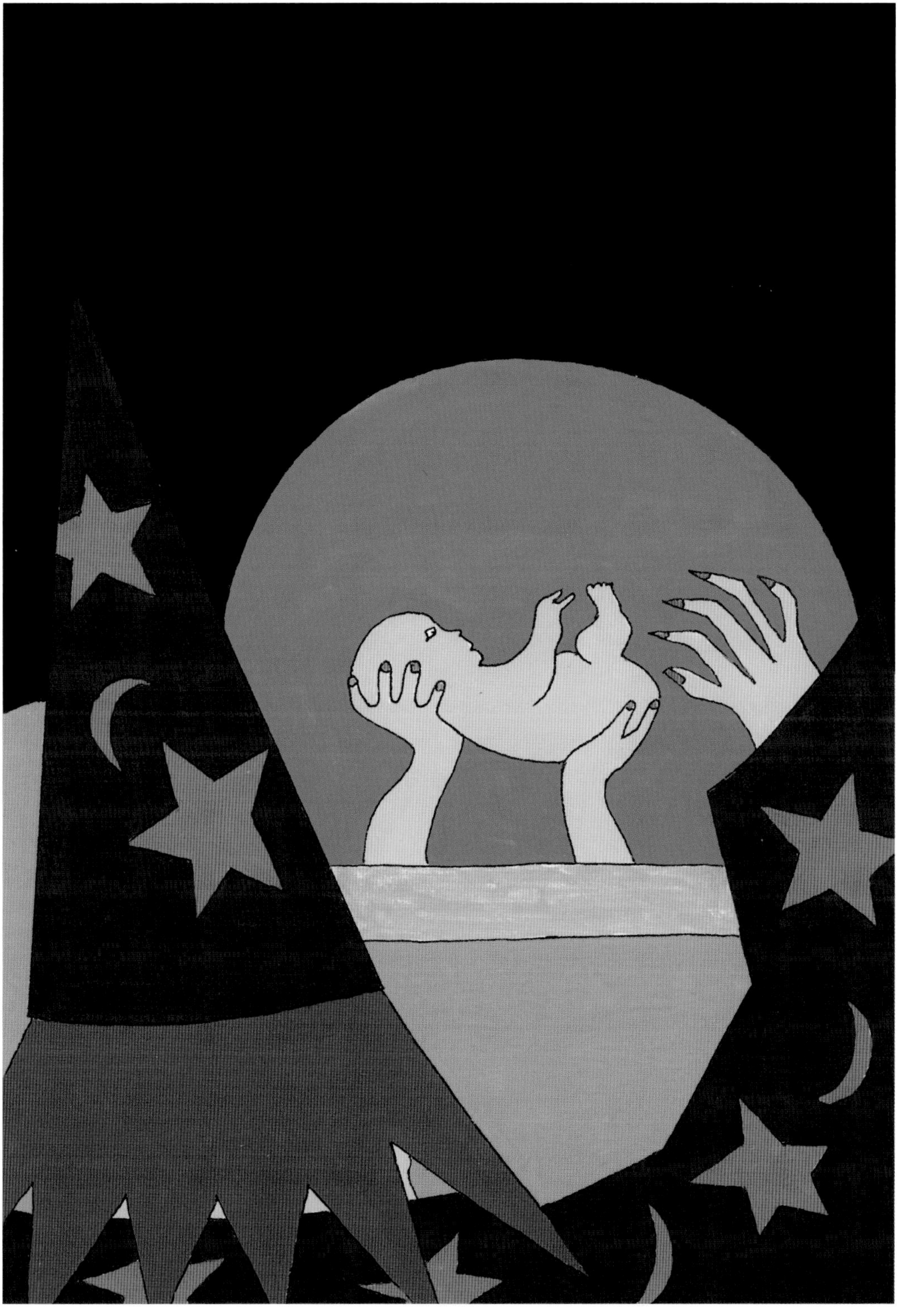

CHAPTER THREE

Griselda might have been given the traditional name of a witch, but she looked like an angel with pretty face, pale golden hair. She should have been the light and joy of her parents' lives, but there was a darker side with temper tantrums, then dark moody silences. Slowly, unseen, the Princess of the Night drew her towards the path of evil, giving her each birthday a special present.

When Griselda awoke early on the morning of her first birthday there was lying at the bottom of her cot a plastic figure dressed as a witch. The little girl loved that figure from the moment she saw it. It glowed in the dark. It hovered in the air and gathering speed soared around the room as Griselda screamed with excitement.

Griselda only had to raise her tiny hand and cry "'itch! 'itch!" and the figure travelled to her. But whenever her parents entered the bedroom the little figure sulked motionless and invisible in a corner. Griselda knew she must keep the figure a secret from her parents and when (hearing her screams of excitement) they came running she smiled and (learning the ways of deceit) pretended all was well.

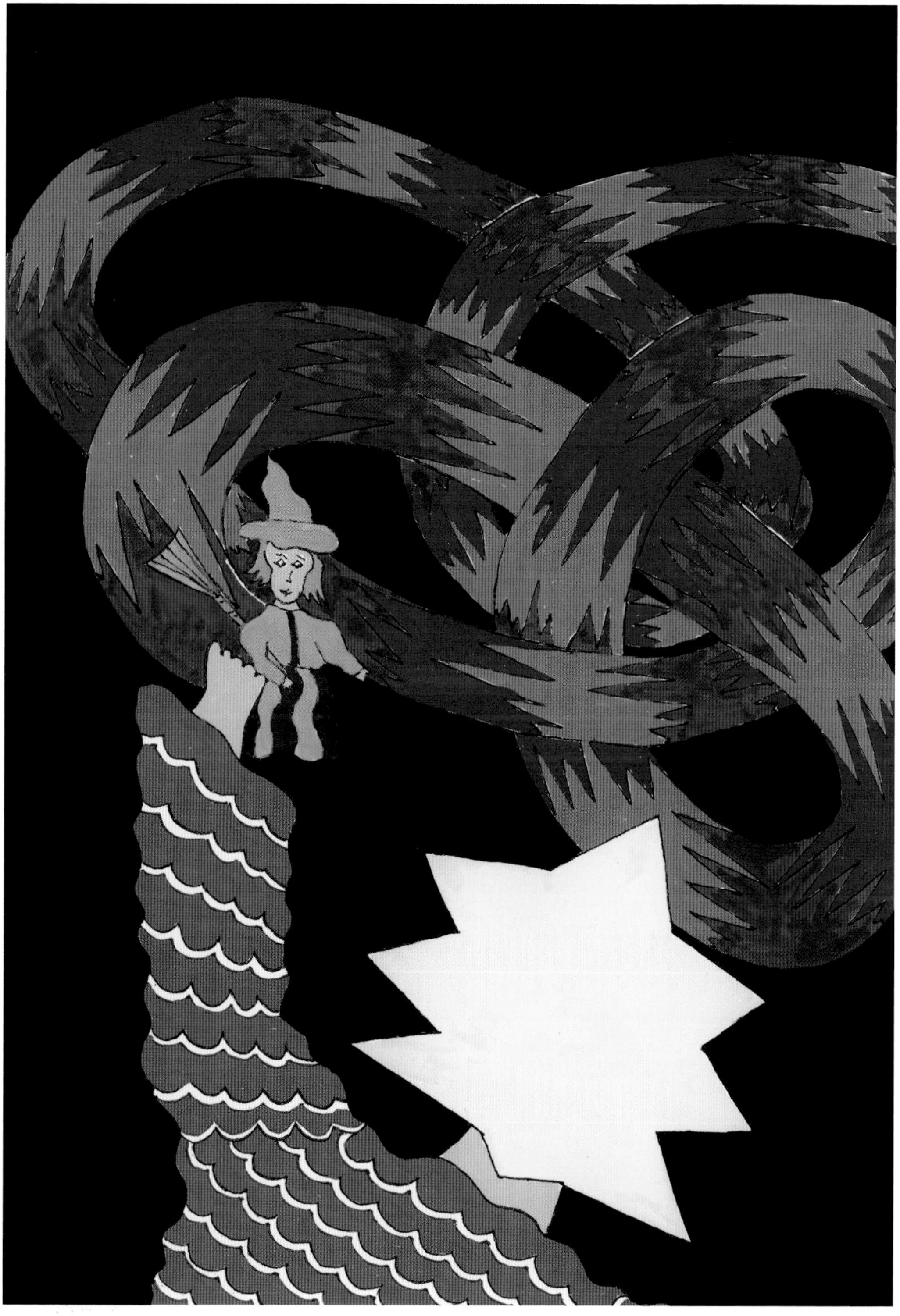

When Griselda awoke early on the morning of her second birthday there was lying at the bottom of her bed a witch's dress of deepest purple with markings of brilliant yellow and a pair little yellow boots. Squealing with excitement she rushed towards the dress and boots, but before she reached them, the dress and boots floated up and dressed themselves upon her.

"Fantastic! So much easier than dressing myself!"

Griselda spun round and glancing in the mirror saw that her hair had turned deep purple to match the dress. "How can I explain this to Mum and Dad?" she wondered aloud.

But Griselda need not have worried. Whenever her mother or father approached her bedroom dress and boots undressed themselves leaving her in her normal clothes with golden hair.

As Griselda grew older dress and boots grew bigger, always the perfect size: more secrets to keep hidden. She looked at herself in the mirror and sighed, "I so much want to grow up and become a proper witch. That would be super!"

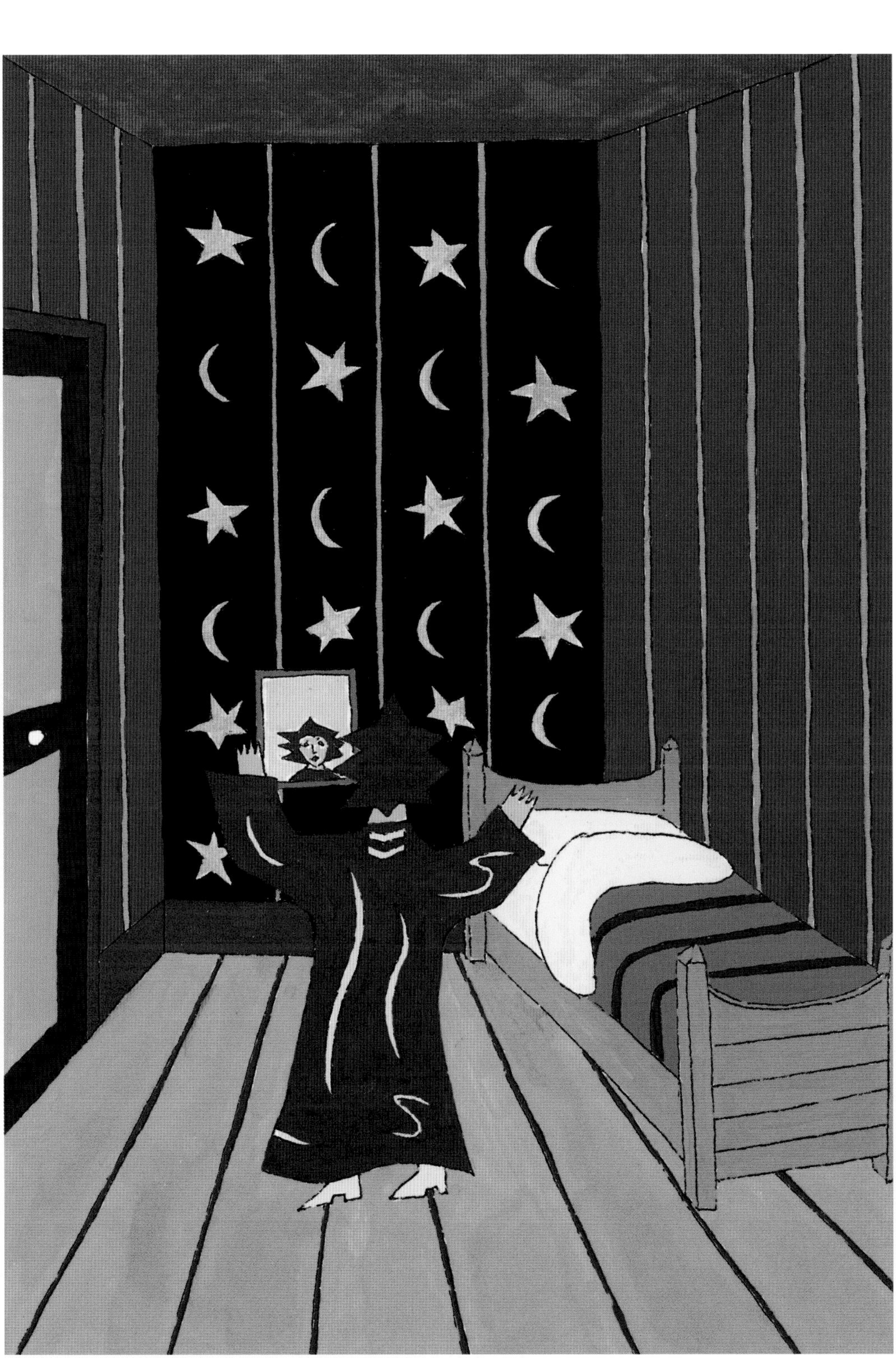

When Griselda awoke early on the morning of her third birthday there was lying at the bottom of her bed a globe of crystal. She cradled it in her hands. It began to hum and moan. Alarmed she put the globe down on the table. Beams of light began to radiate from the globe forming patterns of stars upon the walls and ceiling. Griselda lay upon her bed and looking up tried to identify the constellations which her father had taught her when walking at night across Hayes Common, but none was familiar. Then she realised that her bedroom had grown strangely cold. The ceiling had gone. She was underneath a night sky.

Without thinking Griselda held up a little hand and cried, "'itch! 'itch! What am I looking at?"

"The Galaxy of the Anti-Gods before it was destroyed by my mistress," replied the toy witch.

"'itch! 'itch! You can talk! Why have you never talked before?"

"This is the first time you have asked me a question. But get dressed."

Griselda raised her arms. Witch's dress and boots dressed her. She put the little figure in her pocket and raising her arms once more flew (to her surprise) up into the night sky where before there had been a ceiling. Suddenly she realised she was not alone. The little figure had disappeared from her pocket. She was flying through the night sky hand in hand with a witch who said her name was Garesha.

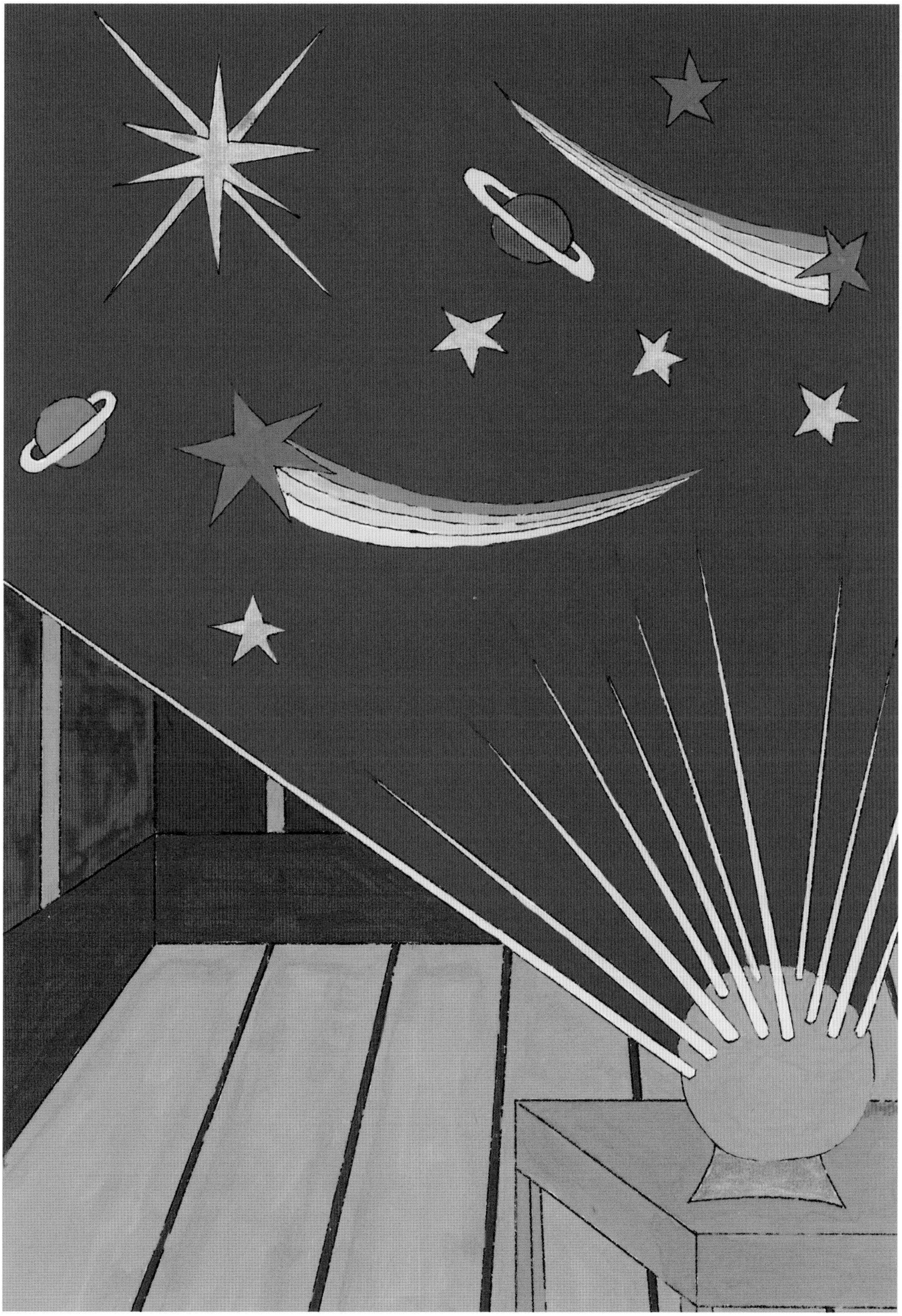

"Where are you taking me?" asked Griselda.

"Back in time to witness the destruction of a galaxy. A sight not seen by many humans. We shall rest on this planet just outside the galaxy. Now watch."

Griselda and Garesha came to rest on a tiny planet of turquoise blue traversed by bands of magenta. The little girl clapped her hands with excitement for something was stirring in the Galaxy of the Anti-Gods. "What is that bright light?" she cried pointing at a distant star.

"The planet Vos where the father of the Princess of the Night ruled as king. It is beginning to glow. It is about to explode."

First the planet Vos, then all the planets in the Galaxy of the Anti-Gods exploded in a searing display of fire and light. At the moment of greatest intensity (when all glowed in pulsating shades of red and yellow) a strange mixture of seething gases passed the little planet with a malevolent whoosh.

"What was that?" cried Griselda startled.

"The Princess of the Night," replied Garesha. "Travelling to earth. Sole survivor of the Galaxy of the Anti-Gods, which she destroyed in a fit of temper at her parents. My mistress. I am a witch of the Order of the Night. Would you like to become one too?"

Something deep inside Griselda was telling her that this was a very bad idea, that she should answer no, but she clapped her hands in excitement and shouted, "Yes! Yes! Yes!"

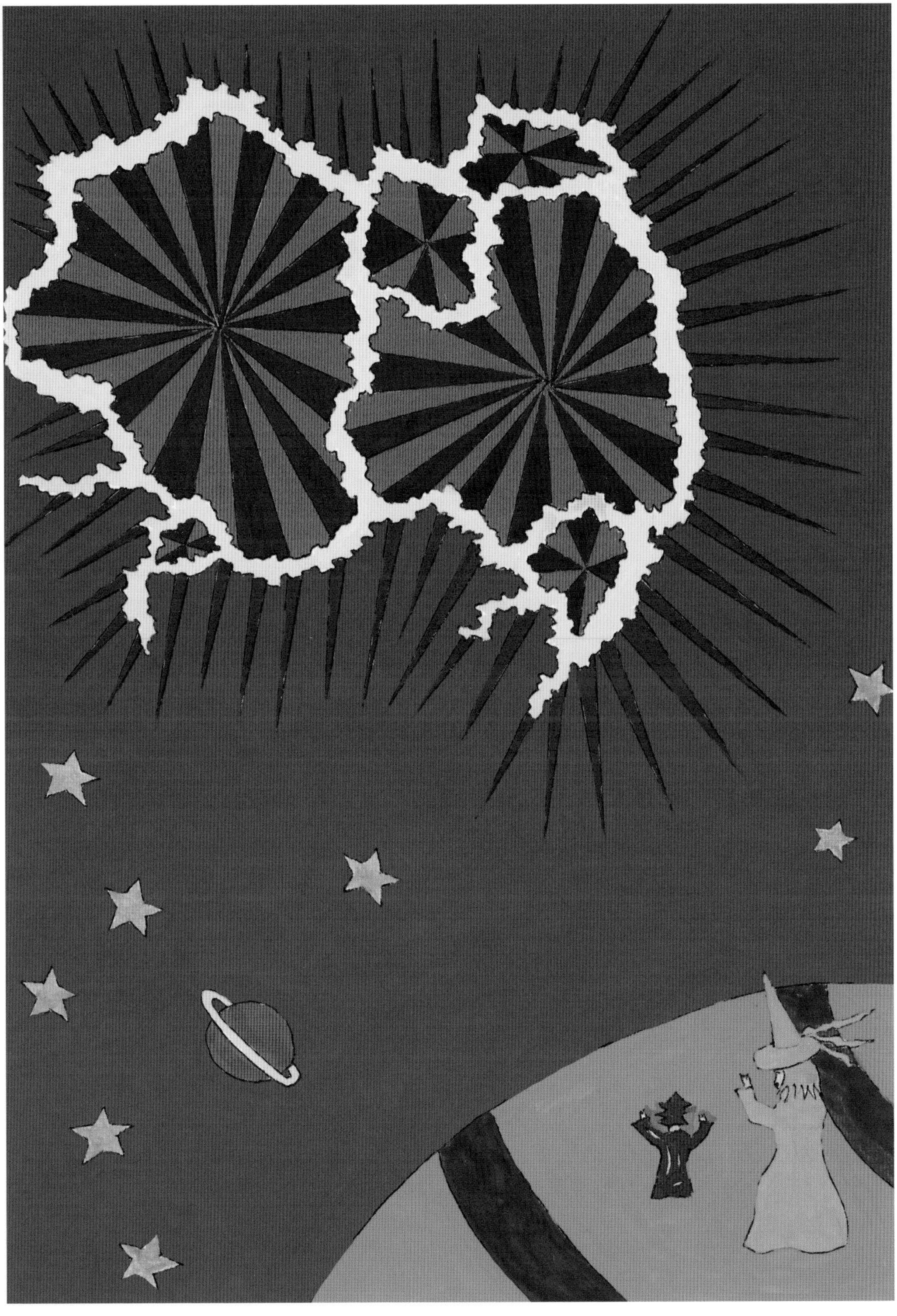

Griselda remembered nothing more before awaking in her bed, cold and frightened. She knew she had done something awful, that the plastic figure had gone forever, that she must never use the crystal ball again. She hid the crystal ball at the back of the wardrobe and ignoring her witch's dress and boots, put on ordinary clothes and shoes and hurried to her mother and father, knowing she could never tell them what was wrong.

Griselda came to a sudden resolution, "I shall be ordinary. No more witch. No more magic." But within herself she knew it was too late.

Griselda did her best to be ordinary, to be normal. She had always been solitary, never mixing with other children, but decided to change. She made friends with a little girl up the road, was invited to a fairy kingdom birthday party, all girls rushing around pretending to be fairies, dancing round a plastic toadstool.

Griselda thought this pathetic. "It's not real! It's so girlie," she spluttered in disgust, as she climbed on the toadstool and broke it.

Griselda never knew why or how it happened, but suddenly as the toadstool cracked in two her fairy costume disappeared and she found herself dressed in her witch's dress and yellow boots with purple hair. She raised her arms and pointed at the little girls.

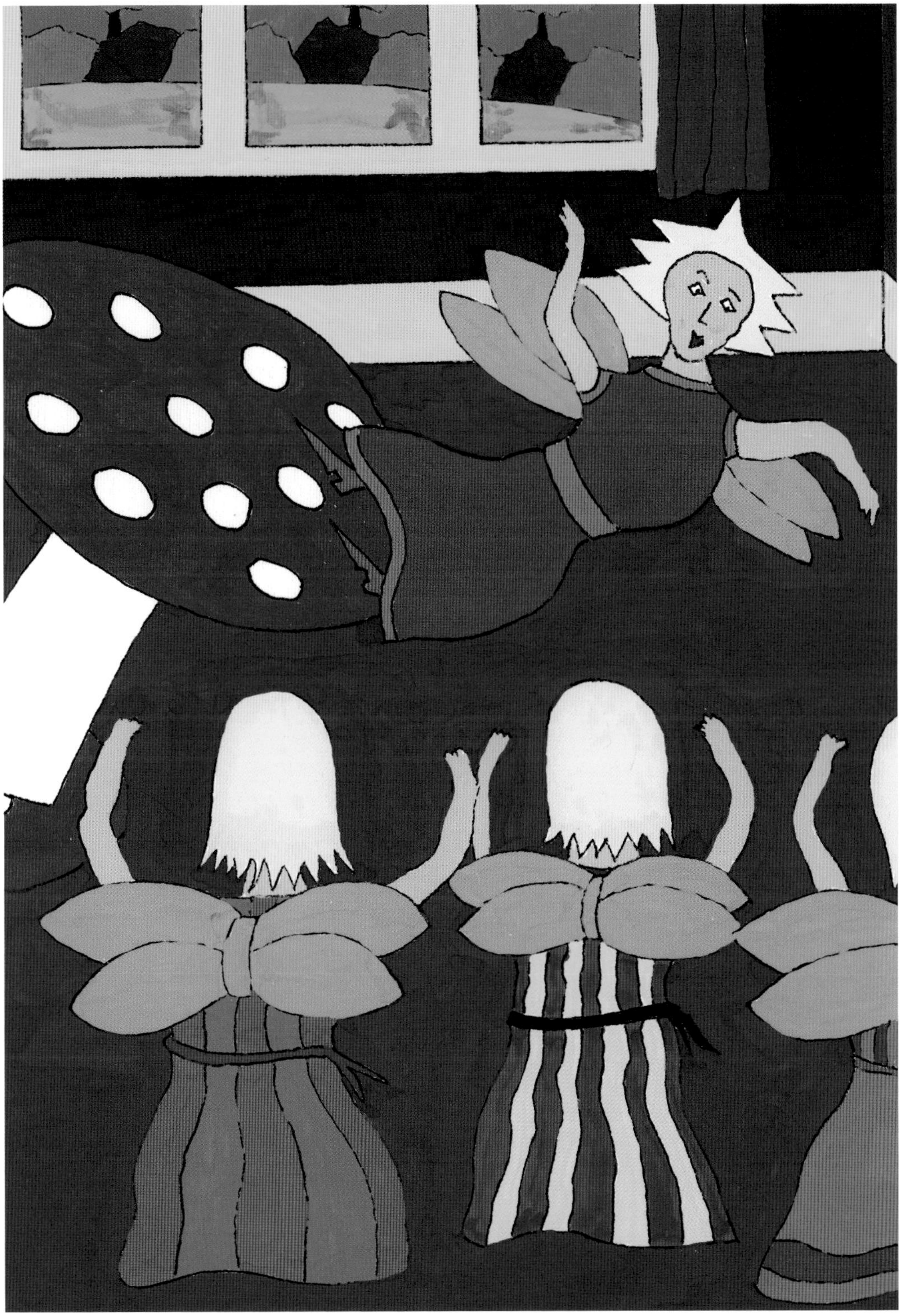

The little girls in their pretty fairy dresses floated into the air, came to rest heads touching the ceiling where they screamed in fear and shouted at the top of their voices, "She's a witch! She's a witch!"

Then Griselda made their fairy wings flap and the girls zoomed around the room like maddened flies until, tiring of the game, Griselda let them drop.

Griselda's mother was summoned. At first it was hard for Melanie to understand what had gone wrong, for by now, whilst all the other little girls were huddled in a corner shaking with terror, Griselda, dressed impeccably with fairy wings and golden hair, was sitting demurely at the table eating raspberry jelly. But when she heard what had happened she took Griselda by the hand, dragged her home and locked her in her bedroom.

As Griselda sat on the bed she could hear her parents whispering. "We should never have had children!" "She is cursed!" "What can we do now?"

After the party no girl in the neighbourhood would have anything to do with Griselda. When she met a girl in the street the girl would panic and flee to the other side of the road. She led a lonely life, but just before her fourth birthday a six–year–old boy moved in next door. His name was Boris.

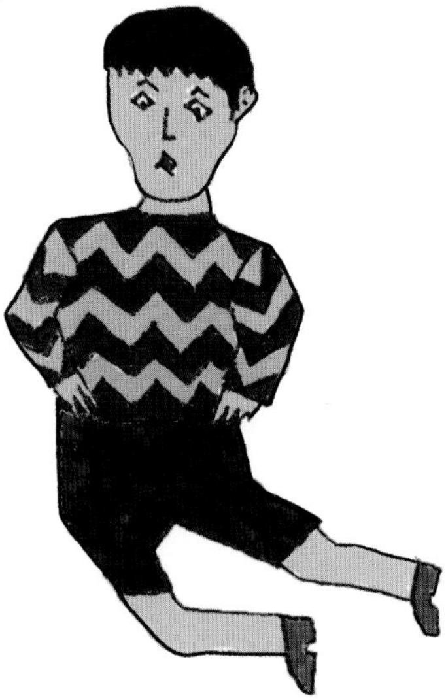

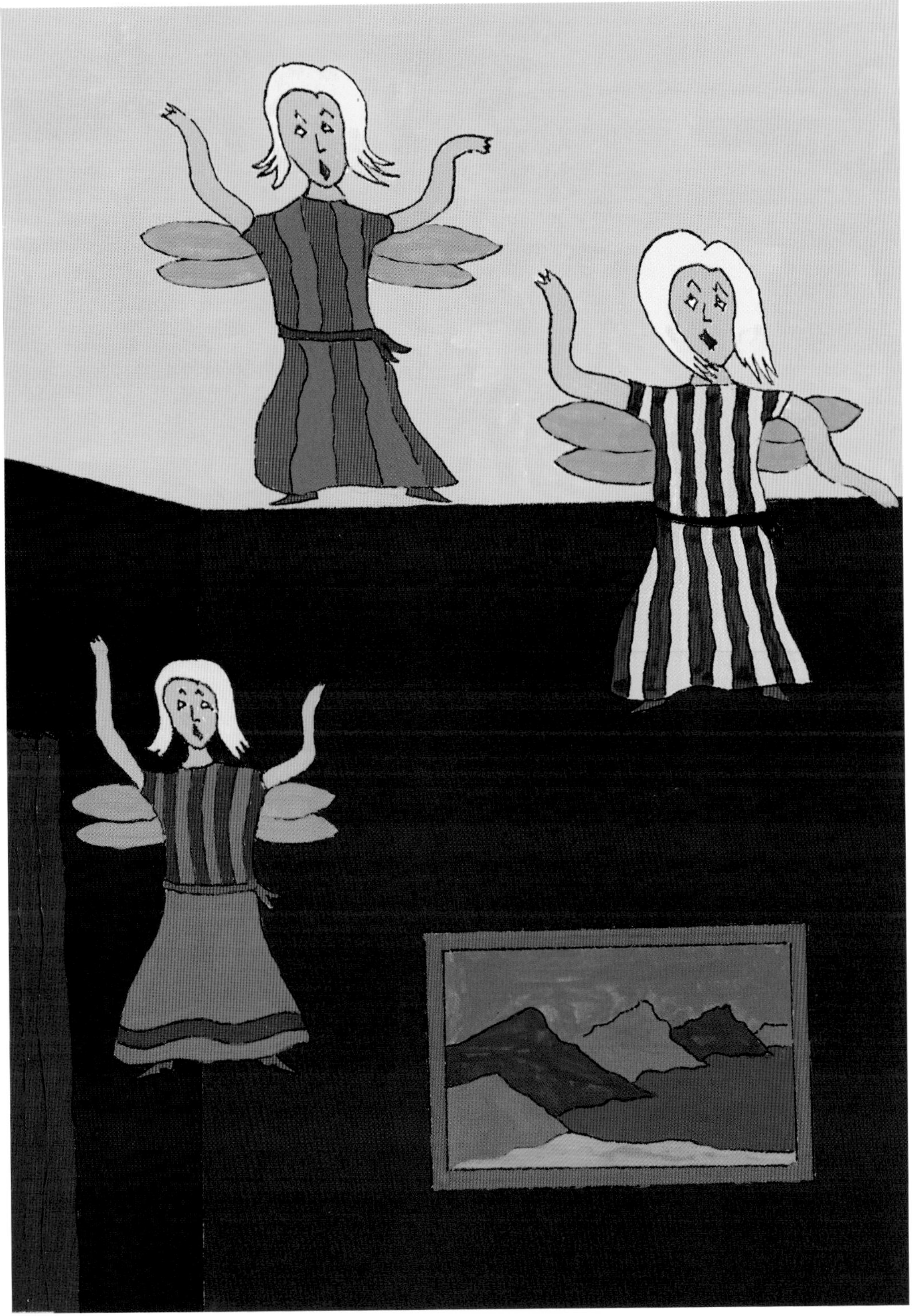

CHAPTER FOUR

Strangely from the moment Boris Austin met Griselda he liked her. Even more strangely she came to like him. Also after the birthday party she realised she really did love magic. She loved the way the pretty little girls floated into the air screaming, "She's a witch! She's a witch!"

"Absolutely brilliant! Fantastic!" enthused Griselda.

Despite being forbidden from doing magic by her parents, on pain of being sent to bed without supper, Griselda wanted to do it again and again. But no girl would play with her. There was only Boris. One day she whispered through the garden fence, "Would you like to play magic?"

"Cool!" replied Boris as he quickly scrambled over the fence and stood before her. She raised her arms and Boris floated into the air. But the boy did not mind at all. "This is great! Put me on top of the garden shed where I can reach those plums high up the tree."

Griselda needed practice. Boris overshot the shed and floated above the fence at the bottom of the garden where the neighbour's dog reared up and tried to bite him. Griselda tried again and with a cry of triumph landed the boy on the shed roof. Boris reached up, picked the ripe fruit and scrambling down joined Griselda. Hiding behind the shed they ate the plums, best of friends.

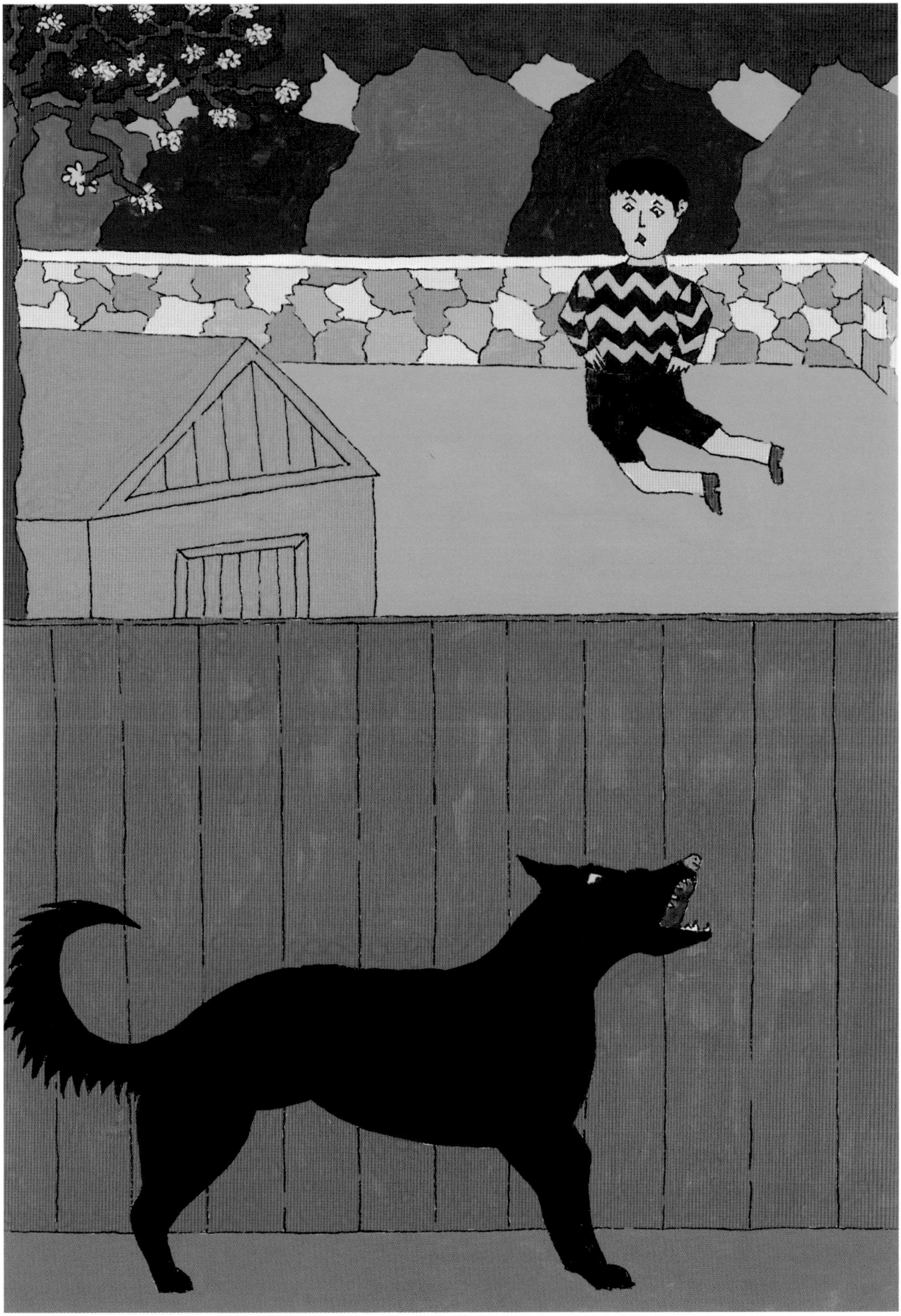

When Griselda awoke early on the morning of her fourth birthday propped up at the bottom of her bed was what looked like a fairy door painted pale green. Griselda looked at it in disgust and spluttered, "How twee! How ghastly! How utterly pathetic!" (at the age of four her command of the English language was well advanced and would change little during later years). She had seen a fairy door at the fairy party. She had read the instructions:

> *"A pretty handcrafted wooden fairy door sprinkled with a little magic, ready for your fairy to move in. Decide where to place your door, then leave the magic key out beside it overnight – if the key is gone next morning your fairy has moved in. All you need to do is believe."*

"Believe!" snorted Griselda. "Pathetic!"

But then she had another thought. Every other birthday present left at the bottom of her bed had been real. Perhaps this was as well. She scrambled out of bed, tore open the envelope sealed with black wax, and read the instructions:

> *"A magic door fashioned by dark powers.*
> *Place against any wall with care, then unlock the door and step inside.*
> *Unsuitable for humans of any age. Use if you dare!"*

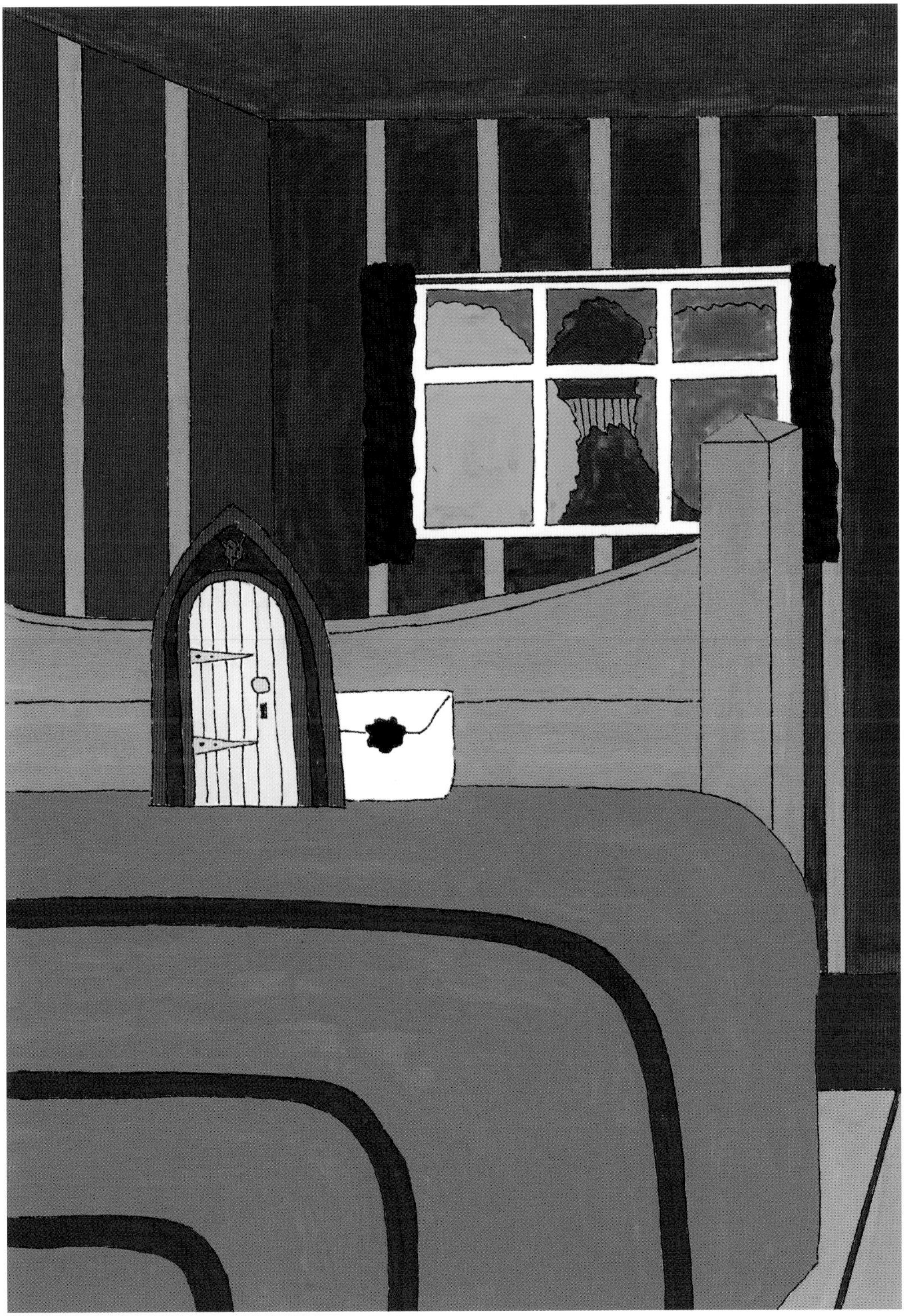

"Cool!" cried Griselda. But after the crystal ball she was cautious. She had been frightened sitting on the tiny planet whilst the Galaxy of the Anti-Gods had exploded. The trip had not gone well. If she was going to go through the door she would not go alone. Boris would come as well.

Boris had not been to Griselda's bedroom before. He was impressed by the witch's dress and boots. One moment Griselda golden haired and wearing pretty dress, the next a witch with purple hair. "Cool!" But when he saw the fairy door standing 10 inches high against the south wall of the bedroom he was not impressed. "I like playing with you Grizel. Even though you are a girl. But I am not doing fairy stuff. If you believe in Tinker Bell, play by yourself."

"But this is real. Hold out your hand."

Reluctantly Boris held out his hand. Griselda took it firmly and bending down turned the key in the lock. They stepped through the tiny door (which seemed strange for they were not conscious of changing size) and found themselves on a sunny beach in the Realm of Ramion. A band of cannibals was running towards them, excited that they had found someone to eat. Quickly boy and girl retreated through the door.

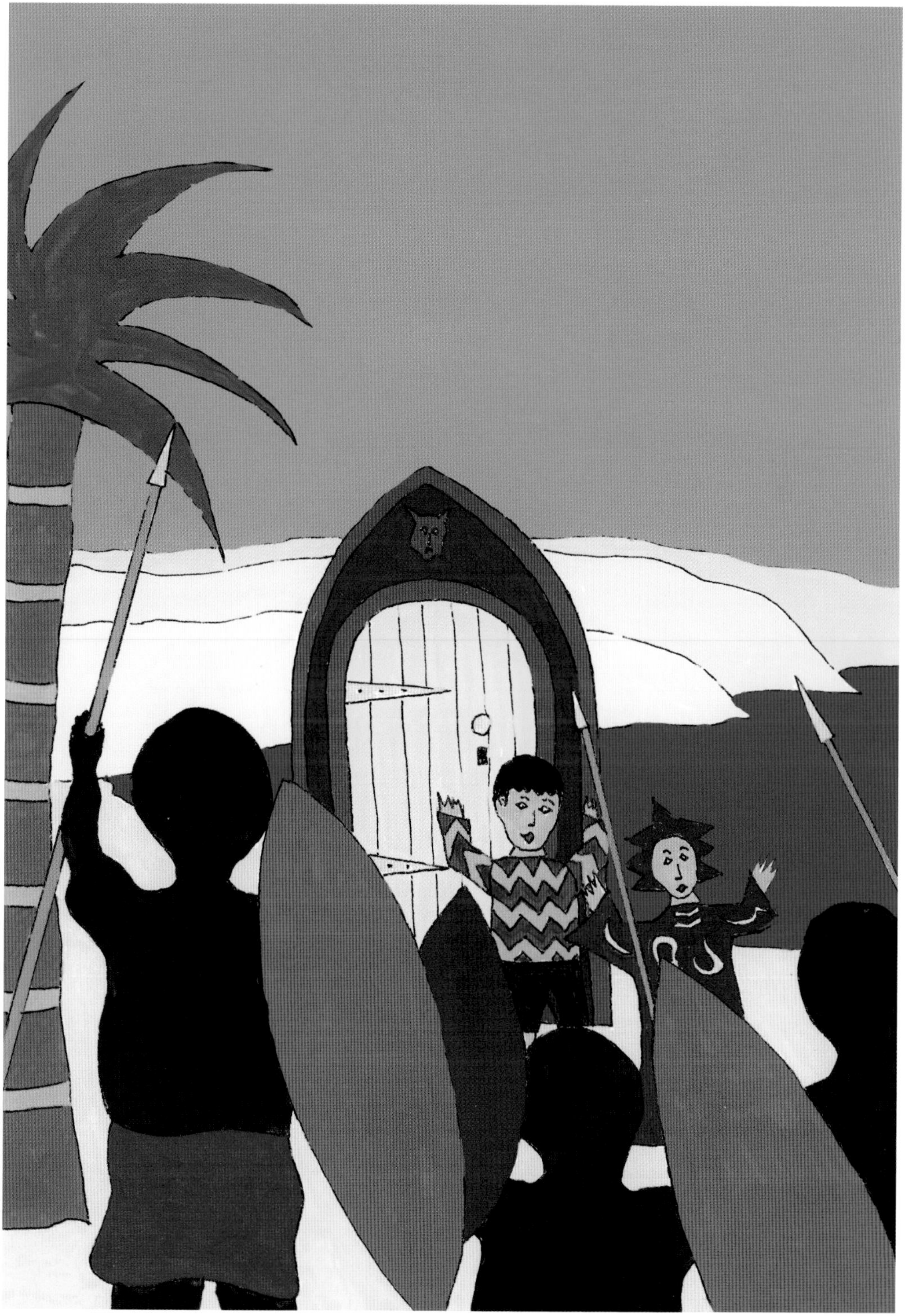

Boris took the instructions and read them carefully. "Place against any wall with care. Use if you dare. They were not joking. Let's try a different wall." He picked up the little door and placed it carefully against the north wall of the bedroom. Then he took Griselda by the hand and stooping down turned the key and both stepped through the door. They found themselves in the icy wastes of Azerstahn in Ramion. Griselda's witch dress immediately grew some extra layers, but Boris was freezing. He started to say, "Let's go back" when he saw a sinister figure standing before them.

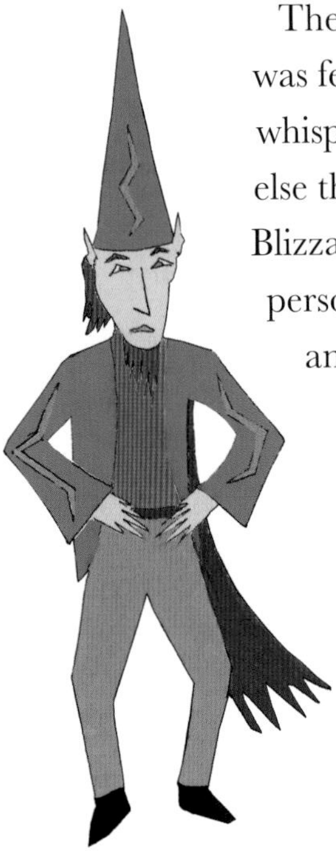

The Blizzard Wizard, with long lanky limbs and evil leer, was feared throughout the Realm of Ramion. Parents would whisper to their children if they misbehaved, "Be good or else the Blizzard Wizard will come and get you!" For if the Blizzard Wizard stretched out his bony fingers and touched a person, he or she would freeze deep inside, and body, mind and spirit turn to ice.

"Welcome!" cried the Blizzard Wizard. "I was told to expect a girl, but I am sure the Princess of the Night will be delighted to get a boy as well!"

So saying the Blizzard Wizard raised his arms, summoned whirlwinds of ice and snow which bound the boy and girl tight and, lifting them up, carried them flying through the air and deposited them in the Sculpture Hall of the Princess of the Night.

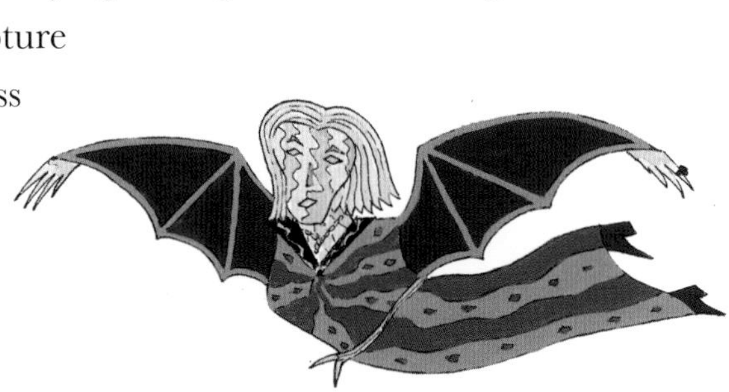

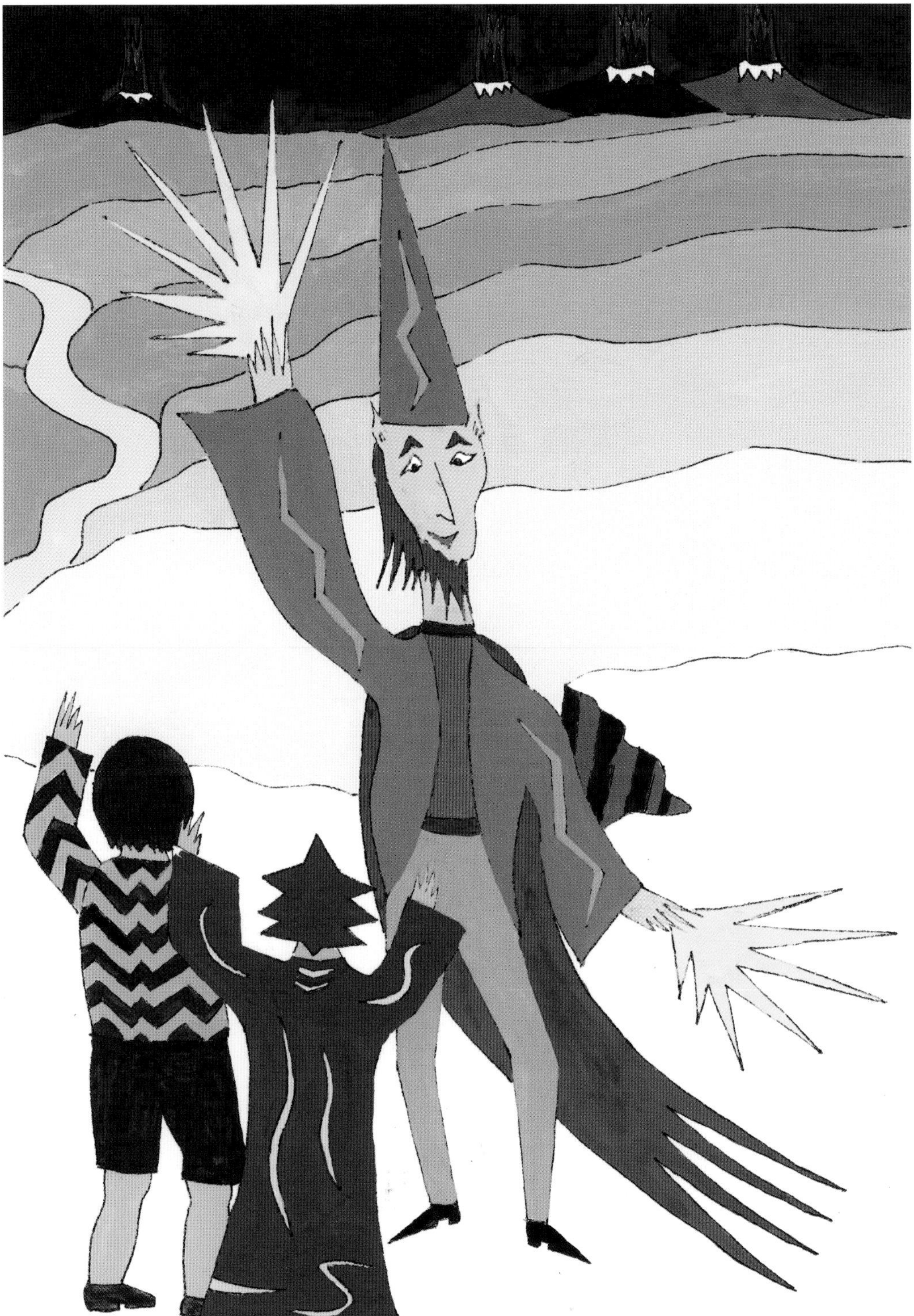

CHAPTER FIVE

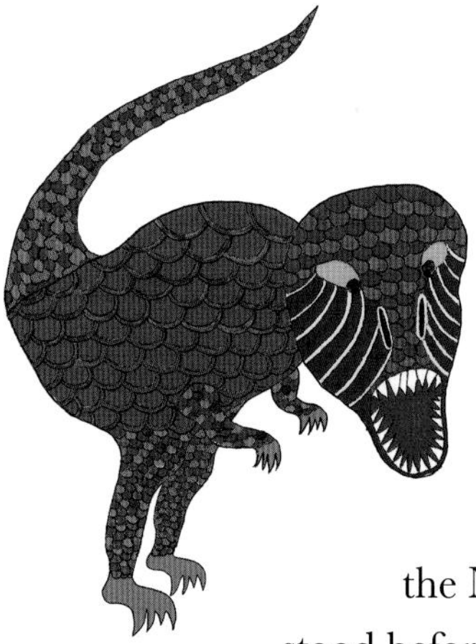

Boris and Griselda looked about them, at the Princess's living sculpture collection: children frozen in the act of playing. Suddenly the Princess of the Night emerged (as if from nowhere) and with her servants stood before them, a hissing mass of malevolence. The Princess stared hard at Griselda. "It is you I wanted, to test you, to see if you are worthy to serve me as a Witch of the Order of the Night. Who is this boy? I have no use for him. I shall add him to my living art collection. What game is he good at playing?"

Griselda ignored the question. She drew herself up high (or at least as high as a four – year – old can do) and looking up into the face of the Princess said firmly, "Boris is my friend. If you want me to be your witch, let him go."

"How sweet!" the Princess sneered. "You care for him. You want to protect him. One day you will not treat him so kindly. You will send thunderbolts to echo in his bony brain. You will kick him out the window."

"That could never be!"

"You will see. I would like him for my collection. But another time. He can take part in the test: I have never tried it on a boy. Then you both can go home (if you survive)."

So saying the Princess raised her magic staff and the boy and girl disappeared.

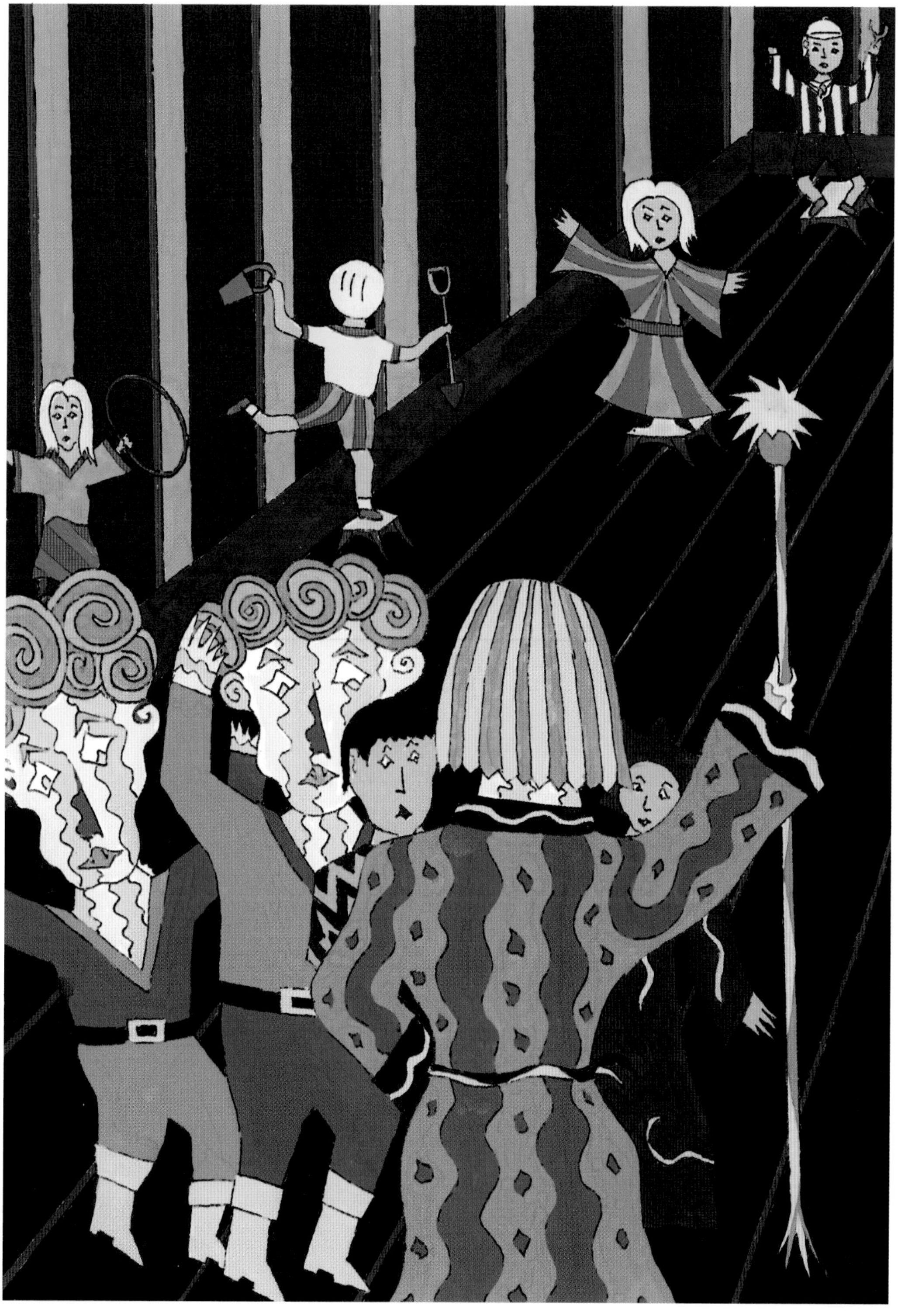

Boris and Griselda found themselves on the rocky hillside in the Realm of Ramion where the mind controls. Griselda had grown strangely agitated. "I won't send thunderbolts to hurt you. I won't kick you. I really won't."

"I know Grizel," said Boris. "We are in this together. We're friends."

But Griselda would not be comforted. Normally so strong, suddenly images of all the things of which she was most frightened came welling up in her mind.

There was a great roar and above a nearby rock rose the head of a Tyrannosaurus rex, turning this way and that, sniffing for blood, chomping its jaws full of razor-sharp teeth. Griselda trembled in terror: she had always been frightened of being chomped by a Tyrannosaurus rex. As the prehistoric monster advanced towards them, suddenly the ground beneath their feet began to ooze and squelch. In a moment of revelation Boris realised what was happening. His greatest fear was being drowned and choked in quicksand: their fears were becoming real.

"Quick! Quick!" Boris cried taking Griselda by the hand, leading her to firmer ground.

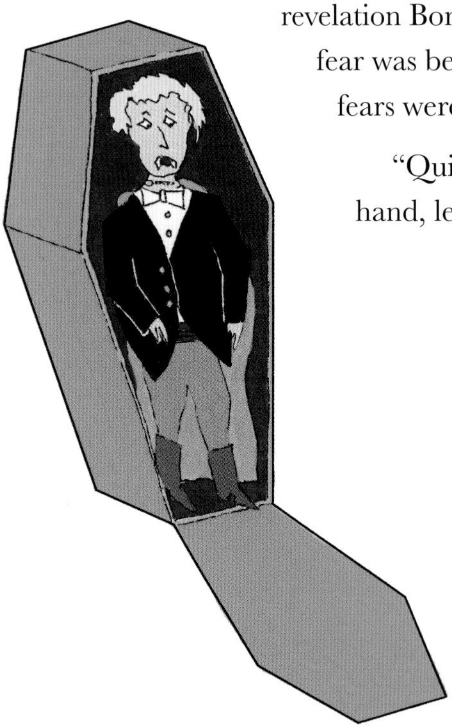

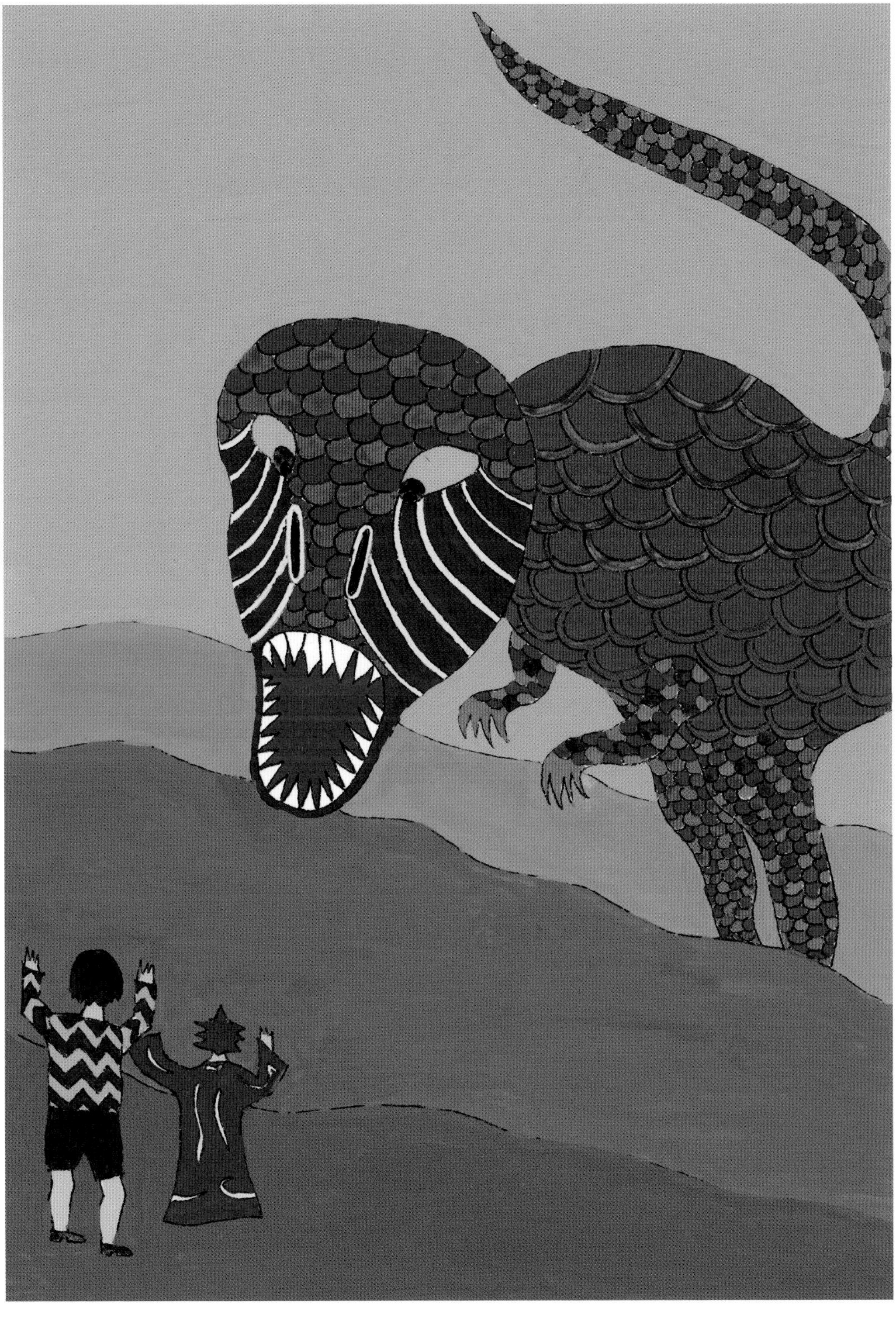

As the boy and girl reached an escarpment of rock they turned round and saw the Tyrannosaurus rex disappear into the quicksand with a terrible roar. But even with the disappearance of the monster Griselda's fears would not be stilled. Suddenly the light vanished and boy and girl found themselves on the rocky hillside in a night of deep shadows and slender moon.

In the moonlight they could see that now they were surrounded by coffins standing up on end. The lids of the coffins fell open. Out of Griselda's imagination stepped vampires licking fangs, longing to suck out the blood of the girl and boy.

"Boris! Boris! Do something. The vampires are going to suck my blood."

Boris was thinking hard of the sun. Slowly the sun began to rise above the hillside. As Boris thought his very hardest the sun rose high into the sky, bathing the hillside in golden radiant light. The vampires recoiled in horror. The one thing they could not stand was sunlight. Hurriedly they retreated into their coffins which disappeared.

"Stop thinking frightening thoughts!" shouted Boris.

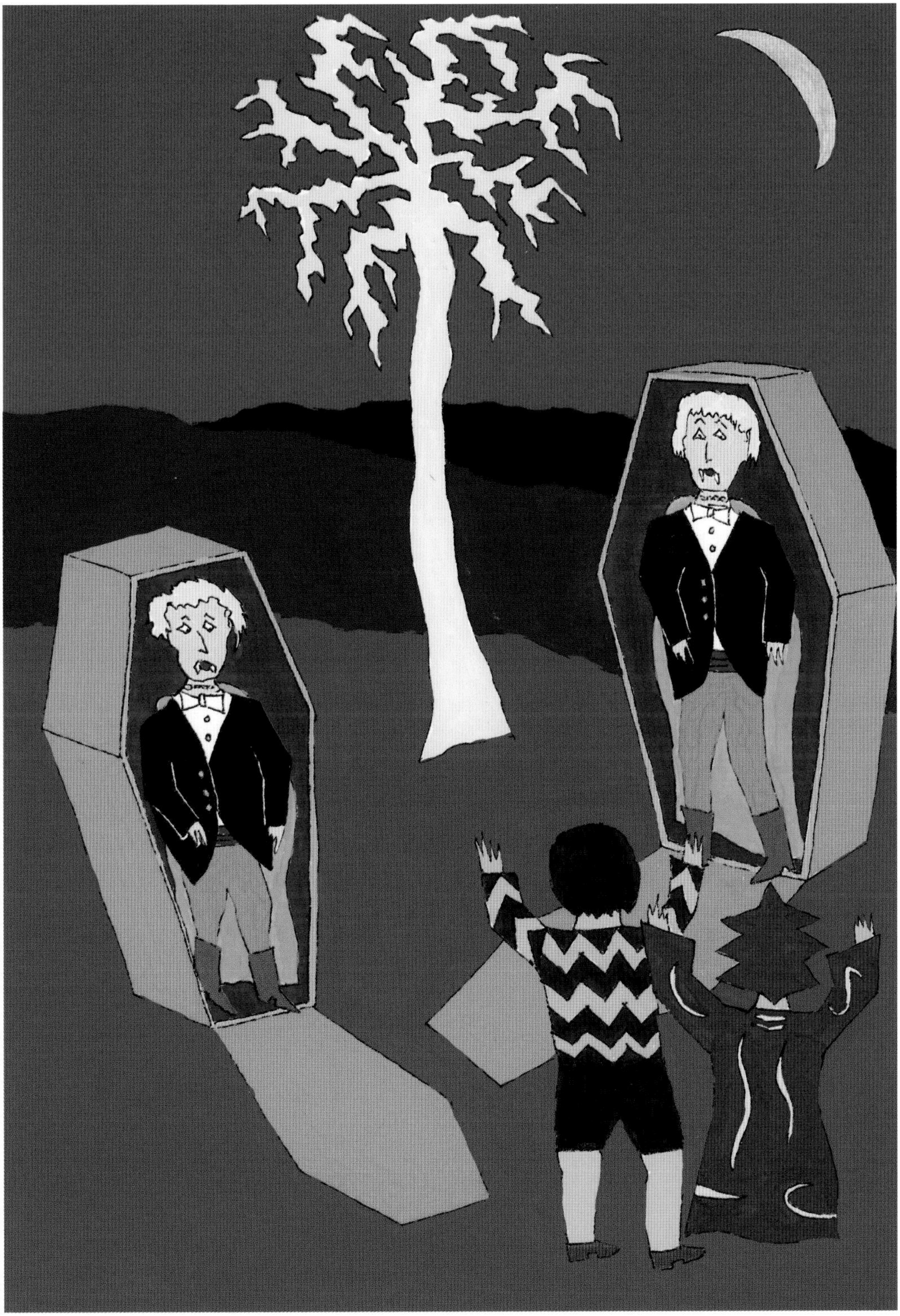

But the words came too late for out of Griselda's imagination came the thing of which she was most frightened. A Tyrannosaurus rex wanting to chomp her flesh was bad, vampires wanting to suck her blood very bad, but to Griselda pigeons were far worse: she had a phobia of birds.

The pigeons which swooped down on Griselda and Boris were no ordinary birds. They were huge with horrid pointy beaks and claws. Lifting her hands to protect her head Griselda froze in horror.

Boris pushed Griselda to the ground and shielded her with his body. As pigeons swooped and soared around their heads he whispered in her ear, "They are coming from your mind. Think of eating plums behind the garden shed."

At the thought of the plums Griselda's mind stilled. Pigeons disappeared and boy and girl found themselves back home behind the garden shed. Griselda clasped her arms around Boris's neck and kissed him on the lips.

"Oh yuck Grizel! Don't be so girlie!" protested Boris (secretly pleased).

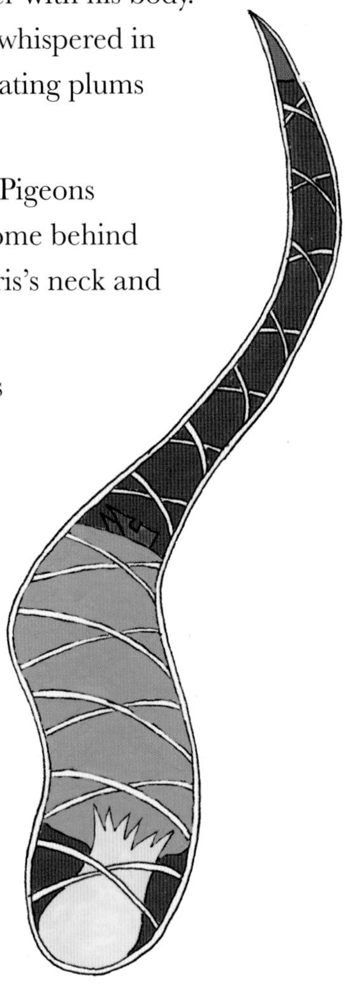

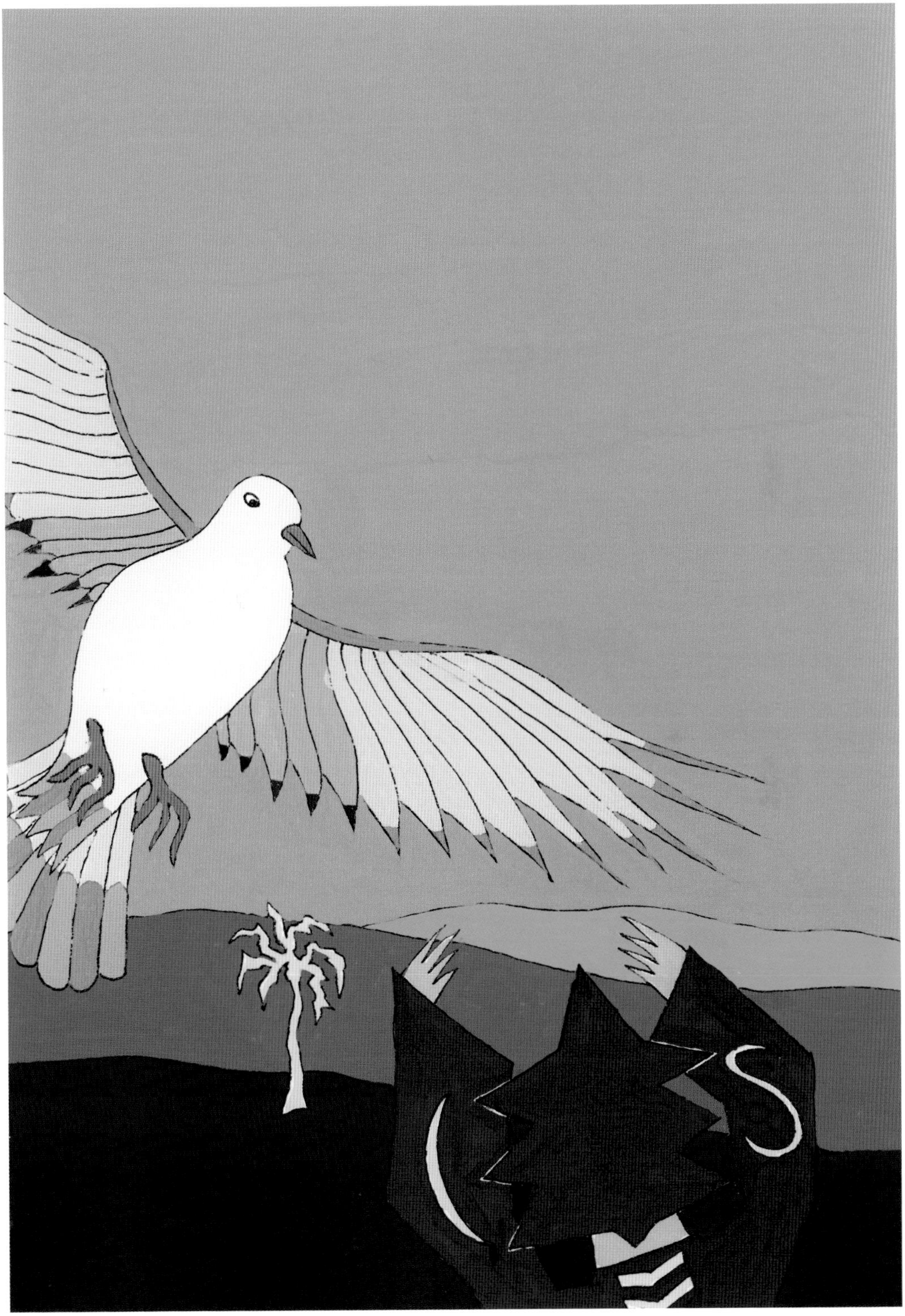

CHAPTER SIX

By magic Sir Tancred kept Griselda and her parents under watch. David and Melanie lived in dread of the day Sir Tancred would come and take Griselda. That day came on the morning of her fifth birthday. Griselda awoke early and looked at the bottom of her bed for her special present. There was nothing there except presents from her parents. She snorted with disgust. When at breakfast her mother asked her whether she liked her doll she muttered, "Yuck!" and went out into the garden. Spying Boris next door she murmured a magic spell and lifted him high into a tree. Boris did not mind at all and hanging upside down from the tree pretended to be a monkey. Suddenly a tall man in sorcerer's robes and hat appeared before Griselda as if from nowhere.

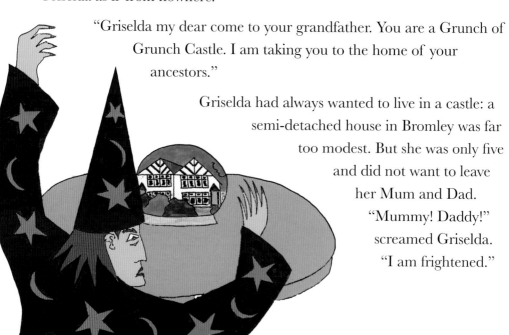

"Griselda my dear come to your grandfather. You are a Grunch of Grunch Castle. I am taking you to the home of your ancestors."

Griselda had always wanted to live in a castle: a semi-detached house in Bromley was far too modest. But she was only five and did not want to leave her Mum and Dad. "Mummy! Daddy!" screamed Griselda. "I am frightened."

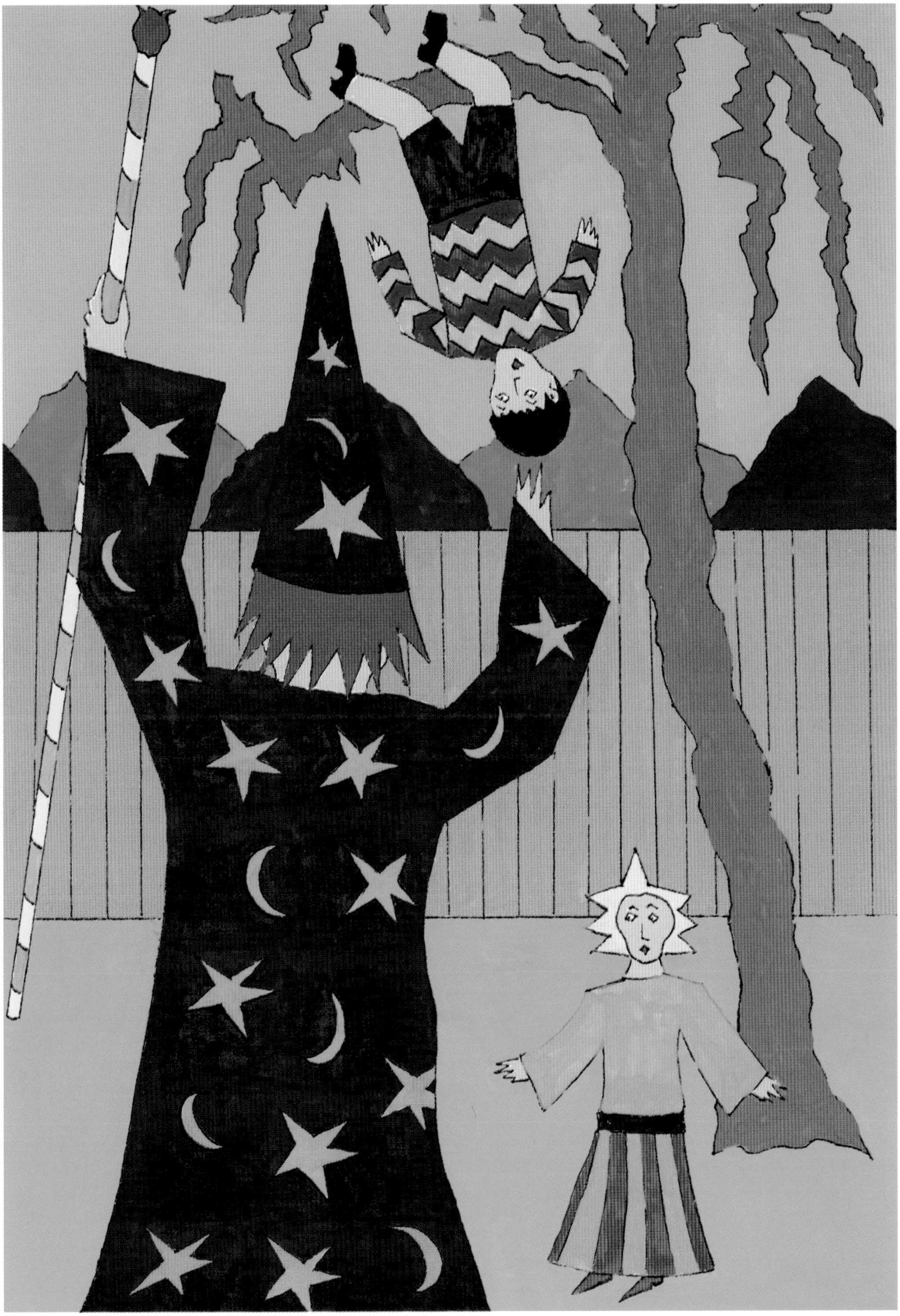

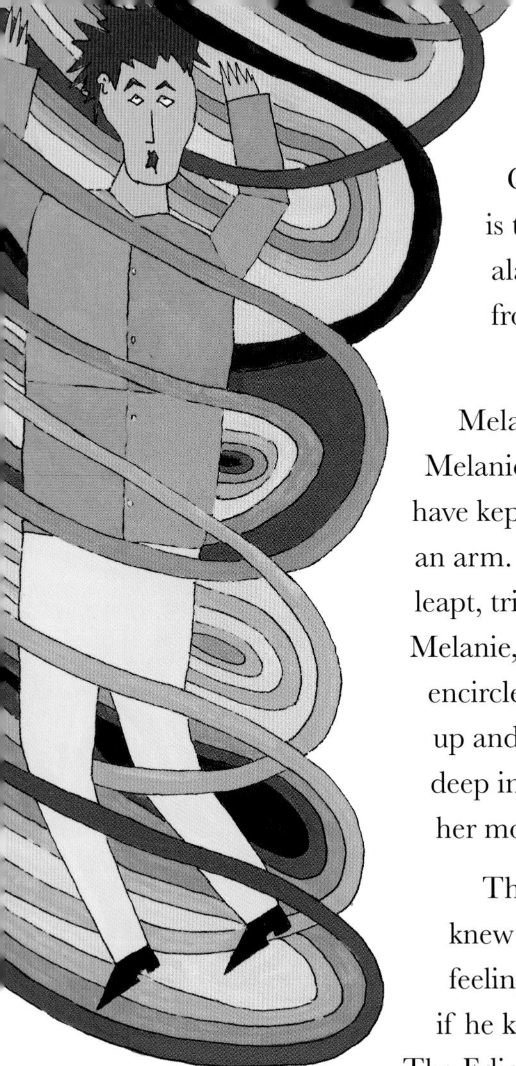

Griselda's parents ran out of the house. "What is the matter?" cried Melanie and David in alarm. Then they saw Sir Tancred standing in front of their daughter.

Melanie's mother had disappeared when Melanie was a baby, before she could teach Melanie the secrets of the white magic which would have kept her safe from harm. Sir Tancred raised an arm. Magic crackled from his magic staff. David leapt, tried to put his body between the magic and Melanie, but nothing could have saved her. A white net encircled her. The ground beneath her feet opened up and as she let out a cry the net pulled her down deep into the earth. Griselda screamed at the loss of her mother. David choked in horror.

Then Sir Tancred turned to his son. Sir Tancred knew that his wife Eveline was weak, that she had feelings for her son, that she would not be pleased if he killed him. But Sir Tancred did not hesitate. The Edicts of the Family Grunch were clear: for a Grunch to marry a descendant of the Wise Woman the penalty was death.

David tried to defend himself. Remembering what his father had taught him he directed all his energy into his hands. With a magic curse he sent laser beams from his index fingers, beams aimed at his father's head.

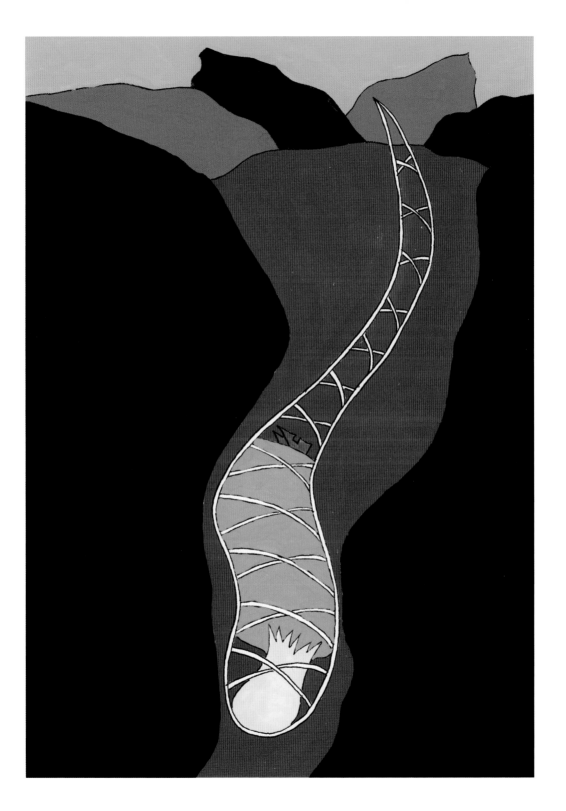

Sir Tancred smiled, a ghastly smile. He was glad his son had learnt something from his lessons, even though not enough. He caught the beams in an outstretched hand and blew them away. Then working deep magic Sir Tancred conjured up a tornado which whirling round David lifted him up into the air and sucked out his life force without leaving a single mark upon his body.

The tornado carried David's body above the streets of Bromley, out across fields and hills until it reached Shoreham. Whirling around the battlements of the ruins of Grunch Castle, howling like a demented banshee, the tornado plunged down into the family vault. Sir Tancred's hunchback manservant Geric was standing ready.

Swiftly he opened the door of a glass tank already prepared to preserve the body in accordance with the Edicts of the Family Grunch. With a final terrible howl the tornado deposited the body inside the tank, then disappeared.

Geric lifted the body up, clicked into place supports beneath the arms, around the chest and following Sir Tancred's strict instructions did not as normal insert a tube into the skull but left it resting on David's scalp. Naturally Sir Tancred did not want the good in David bubbling up and contaminating the evil spirit. Then Geric turned a tap. The tank slowly filled with preserving fluid.

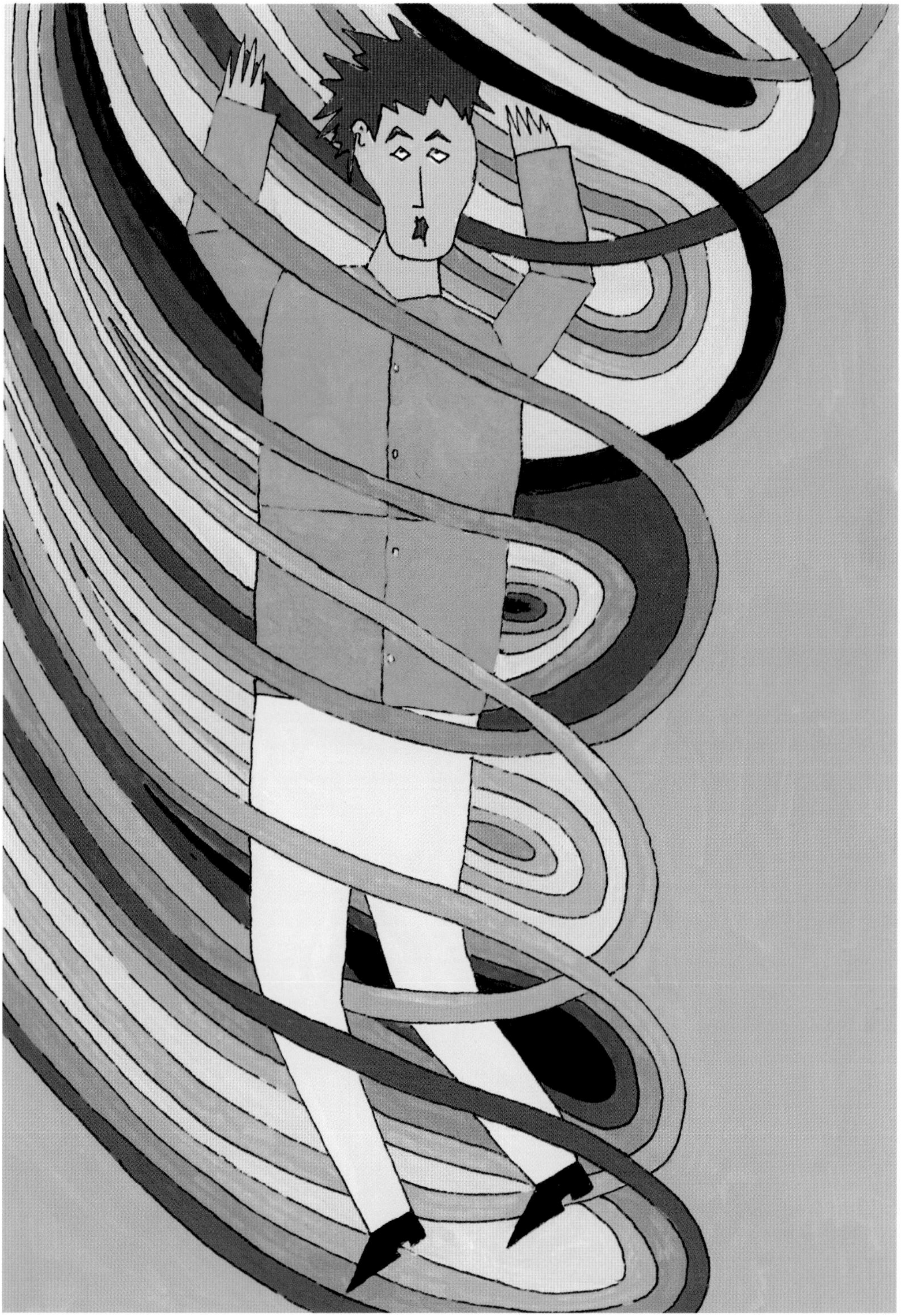

Back in the garden as David's body was carried off Sir Tancred turned to Griselda. Stooping down he picked her up and placed her screaming body over his shoulder. At that moment Boris dropped from the tree. He flew at the sorcerer, arms outstretched, fists clenched. "Griselda is my friend. Let her go! Let her go!" Boris shouted as he pummelled his little fists on the sorcerer's chest.

Sir Tancred raised his arm and with a single blow sent Boris flying into the bushes. The boy scrambled to his feet and flew once more at the sorcerer. "Enough!" cried Sir Tancred, as raising his arm a second time he placed a force field between them. Ignoring the pain Boris banged his fists again and again on the force field and shouted, "Griselda! Griselda! I will never leave you! I will find you! I will save you!"

"I think not," replied Sir Tancred. "If I see your miserable little face again you will regret it." So saying he raised his arm a third time and disappeared with Griselda.

At the memory Sir Tancred stirred in the glass tank. "That boy Boris! His love for Griselda! Her love for him! What trouble it has caused! I should have killed him when first I saw him."

On Sir Tancred's return to Grunch Castle his wife was not pleased to see him. She took one look at Griselda lying frightened on the ground where Sir Tancred had dropped her and knew at once that the girl was her granddaughter. "What have you done? Where is David?"

"As the Edicts of the Family Grunch decree. In the vault. With his ancestors."

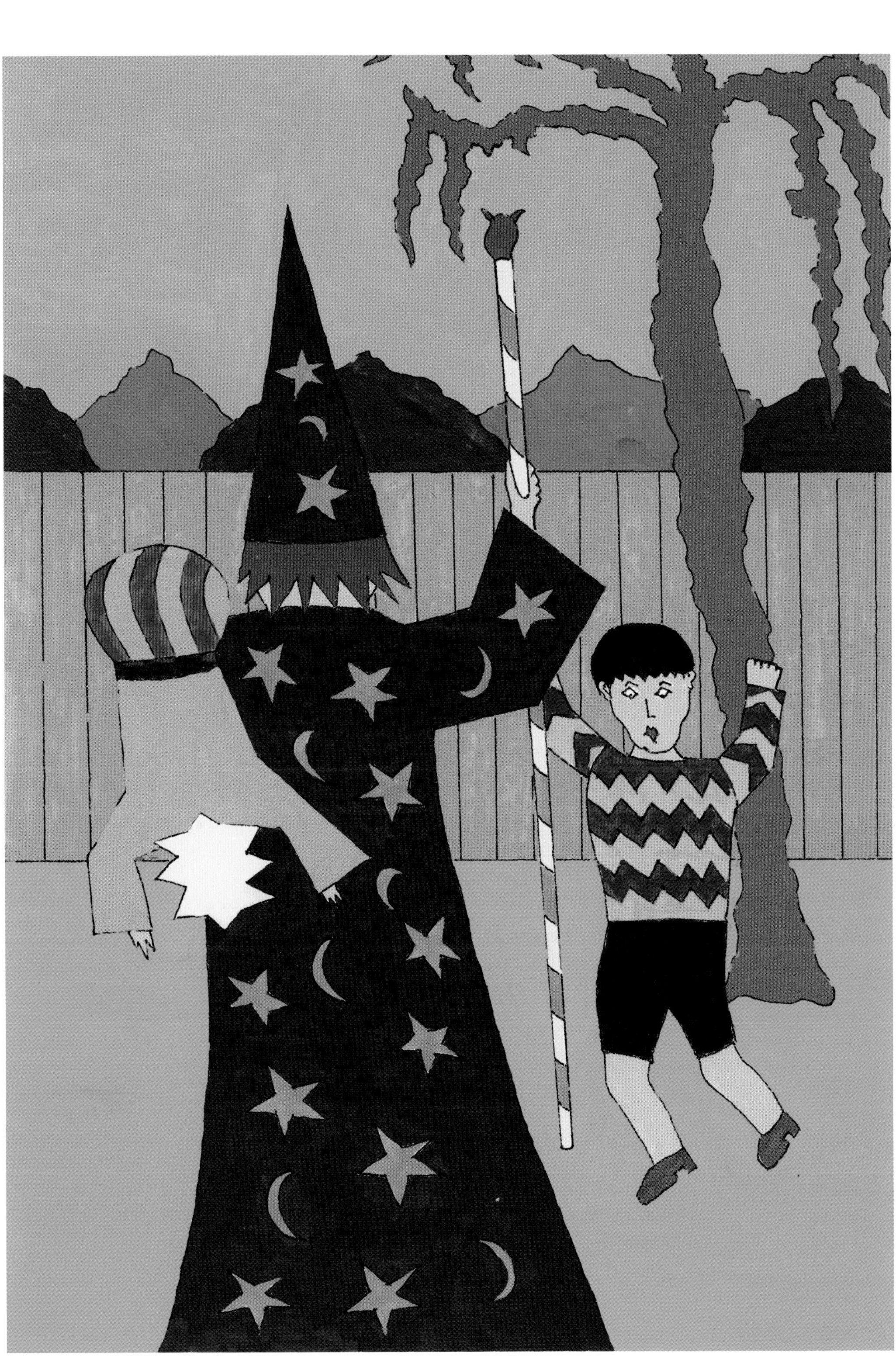

"You've killed him!" screeched Lady Grunch flying at her husband talons outstretched. Sir Tancred had expected trouble from his wife. He had prepared a sleeping potion. As she flew at him he opened his fist and blew the potion in her face. Eveline yawned, tumbled to the ground and fell asleep.

Griselda had run out of tears, had stopped screaming. She scrambled to her feet, and looking hard at Sir Tancred cried, "One day Boris will come and rescue me. Then you will be sorry."

At this Sir Tancred laughed. "That pathetic child. You make me laugh. But you have had your first lesson in the ways of evil. You want revenge. You feel hatred. Of that I am glad. My manservant Geric will show you to your bedroom. We will continue your lessons in the ways of evil another time." Geric stepped out of the shadows and taking Griselda by the hand dragged her off to a bedroom at the top of the tower. He locked the door.

Inside Griselda found her bedroom magically transported from her parents' home to the castle. On the bed lay two books, her birthday present from the Princess of the Night: The Collected Works of Hans Lucifer Andersen (whose stories were changed by his son Hans Christian to make them acceptable to the general public) and Tales of Shadow by The Sisters Grimm (delinquent younger sisters of the Brothers Grimm). The Tales of Shadow fell open at the story of Hansel and Gretel. Griselda had only just begun to learn how to read, but as she looked at the story words rose up from the page and sounds and images began to dance inside her mind. The pages of the story turned by themselves and as they did so all memories of her mother and father vanished. At the end of the story she clapped her hands in glee. "The witch ate the children! A witch! That's what I want to be when I grow up!"

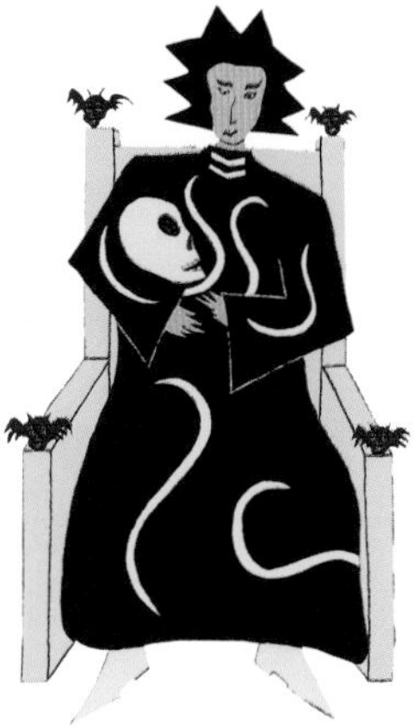

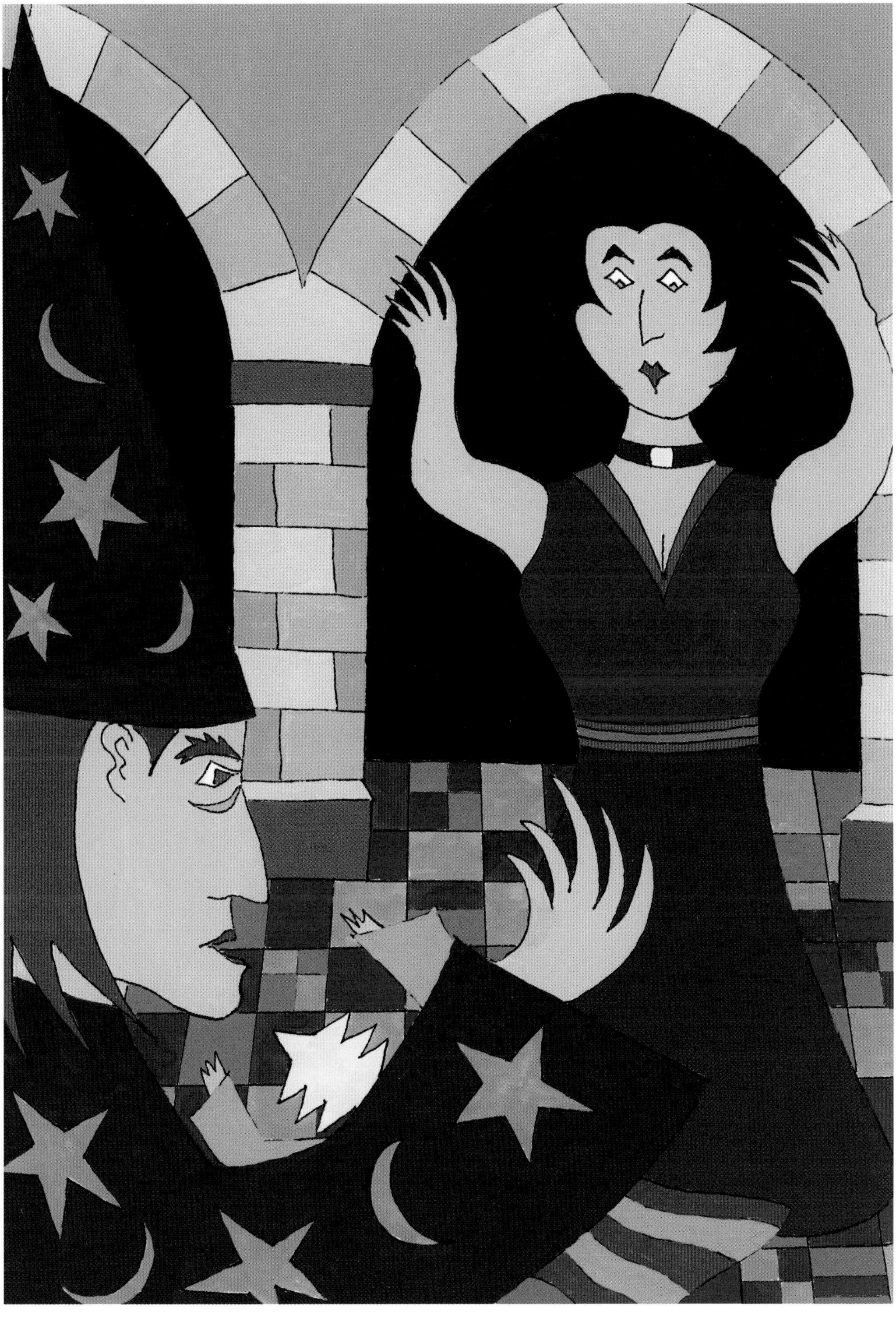

CHAPTER SEVEN

Despite the birthday gifts Griselda's lessons in the ways of evil did not start well. Being of a contrary nature she refused to wear her witch's outfit. She sat upon her bed with golden hair, in pretty dress trying (without complete success) to look like an angel. When Sir Tancred saw her he exploded, "No food and drink for you, young lady! You will stay locked up in your bedroom." At this Griselda stuck out her tongue. Then in the evening of the second day Sir Tancred went to see Griselda with a glass of evil spirit and a tray of food. "Drink this Griselda," cried Sir Tancred holding out the glass of evil spirit. "Then you can have this tray of food."

Griselda took the glass. She sniffed the liquid. The horrid smell stuck in her throat. She stamped her foot and cried, "Shall not" and threw the glass and liquid out of the window.

"Then you will have nothing to eat."

This happened for 10 days. Each evening Sir Tancred came with tray of food and glass of evil spirit. When asked to drink Griselda would throw the glass out of the window and sometimes (when she was feeling particularly feisty) would grab the tray and throw that out as well. Sir Tancred was puzzled. Griselda kept refusing food and drink and yet was not wasting away. Indeed, she seemed in the very best of health and spirits.

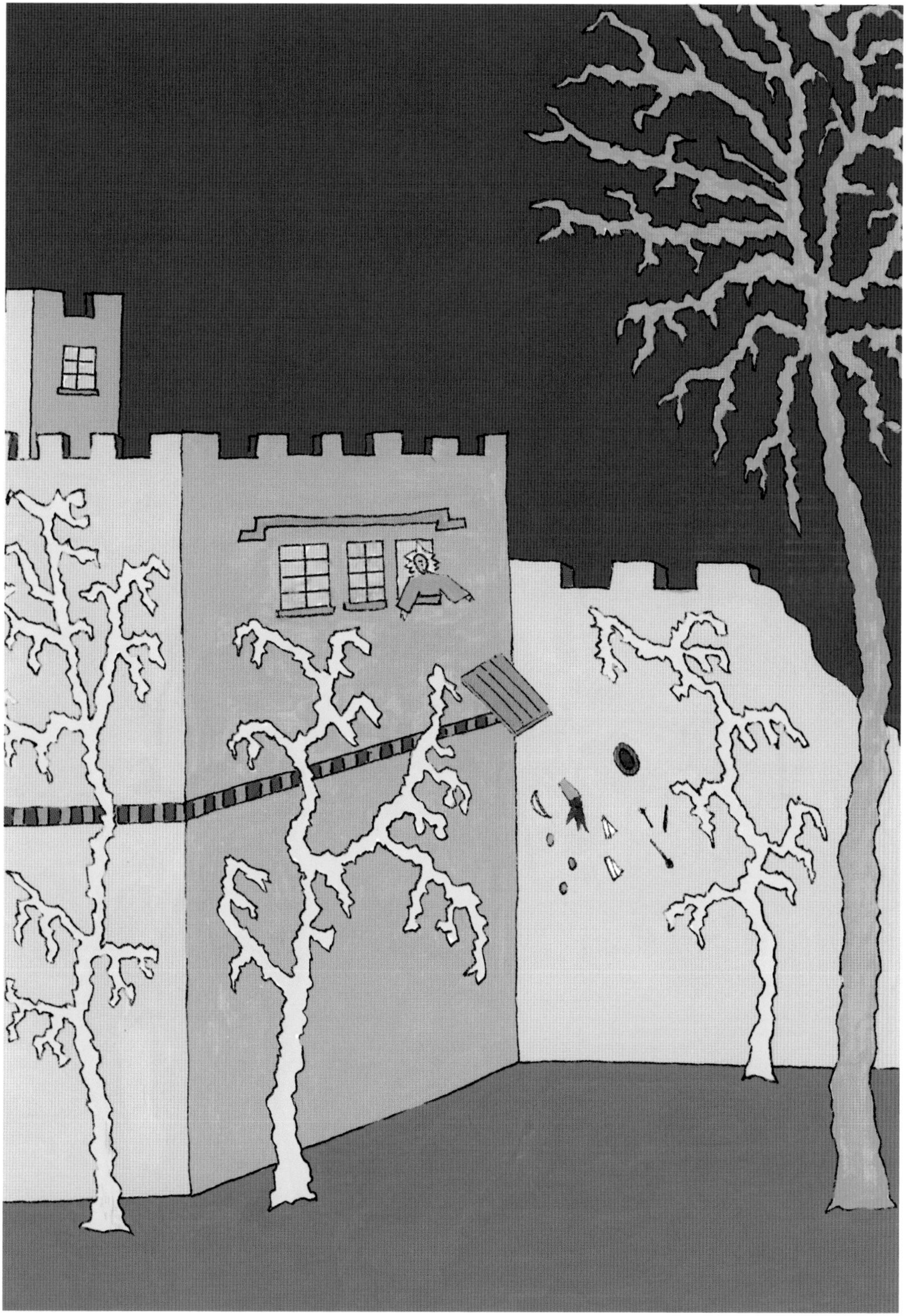

Sir Tancred stood in the corridor outside the bedroom deep in thought. "Something is wrong," he murmured to himself. "I must find out what."

Muttering a magic curse Sir Tancred disguised himself as a spider, scurried under the bedroom door, crept onto the top of the wardrobe and waited. In the middle of the night, when all should have been fast asleep, the door creaked open. In crept Lady Grunch carrying a tray of food and drink (ginger beer not evil spirit).

"Great!" cried Griselda. "I am glad to see you Granny. I am really hungry. Do you know how long I am going to be kept locked in here?"

"No idea," replied her Granny. "But do not worry about that great big nasty. I'll make sure you are fed."

"Great big nasty!" squeaked the spider as Sir Tancred, shaking with anger, fell off the wardrobe, landed on the floor and turned into his normal self. "How dare you interfere with my care for Griselda."

"Care! Care!" bellowed Lady Grunch. "How dare you neglect my granddaughter." Her voice was so loud even Sir Tancred trembled.

"Very well. You may feed her, but she must learn the path of evil. I shall try another way," he added as he raised his arm and magicked Griselda to the Place of Nightmares.

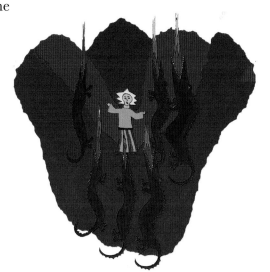

68

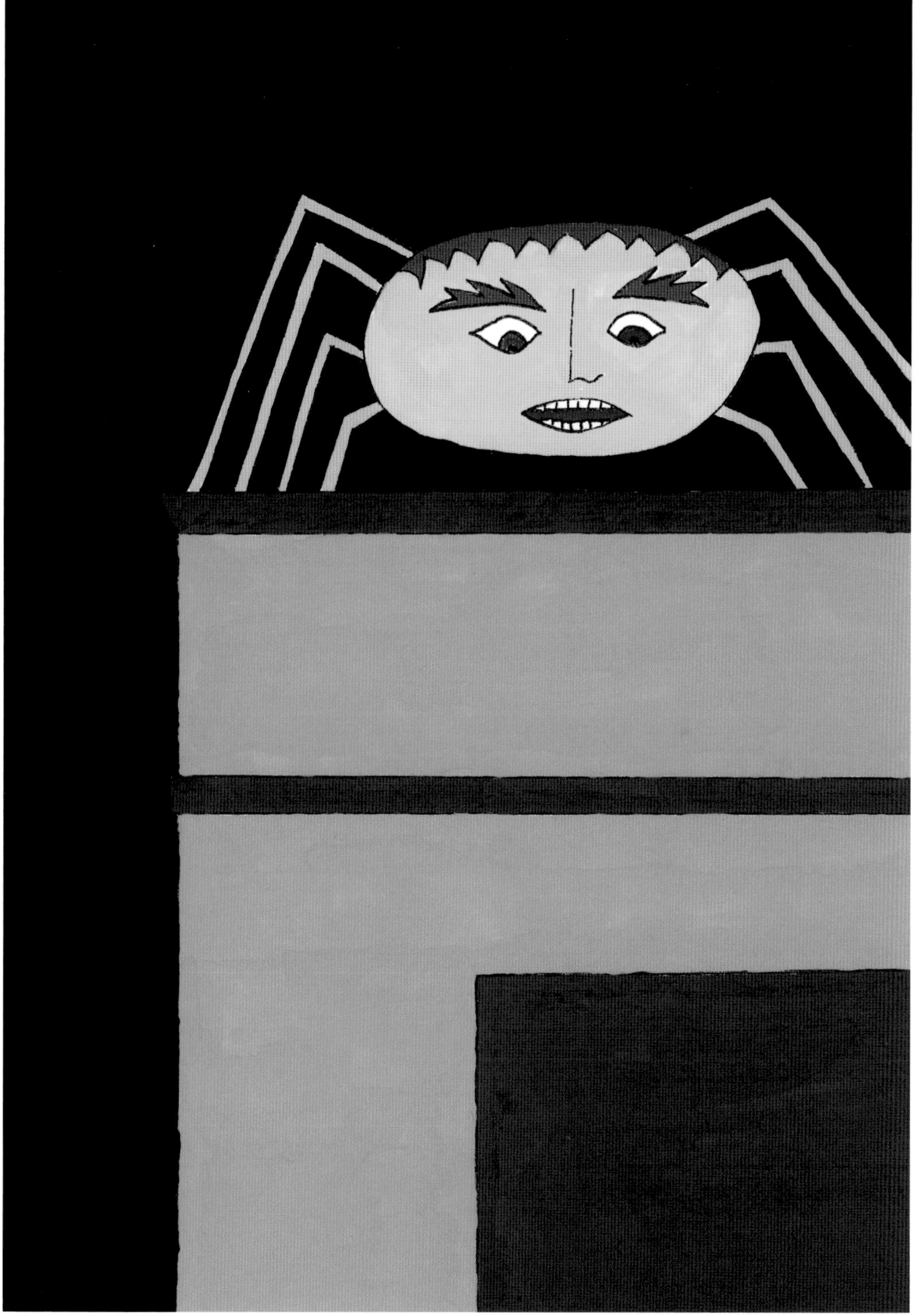

Griselda did not enjoy the Place of Nightmares. Landing in a forest the ground opened up beneath her feet and she plunged down into a fiery pit where alligators of liquid fire danced upon their tails and breathed out flame.

Then as Griselda screamed in terror she found herself flying through the air surrounded by huge man-eating birds each trying to bite off her head. Next moment she was deep in a jungle where snakes bent down from every tree and tried to wind themselves around her neck.

As Griselda ran between high rocks Sir Tancred stood before her holding out a glass of evil spirit. "Drink this and I will take you back to Grunch Castle."

But Griselda was an intelligent girl. She had quickly realised that in the Place of Nightmares nothing was real, that if she did not panic she would come to no harm. "Shall not," she cried dashing the glass of evil spirit to the ground. "Nothing here is real. Leave me here. I do not care. I hate you."

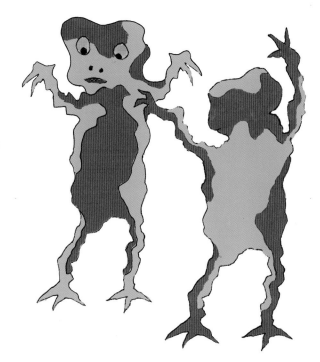

Sir Tancred bellowed in anger. Raising his arm he transported her to the Kingdom of the Frogs.

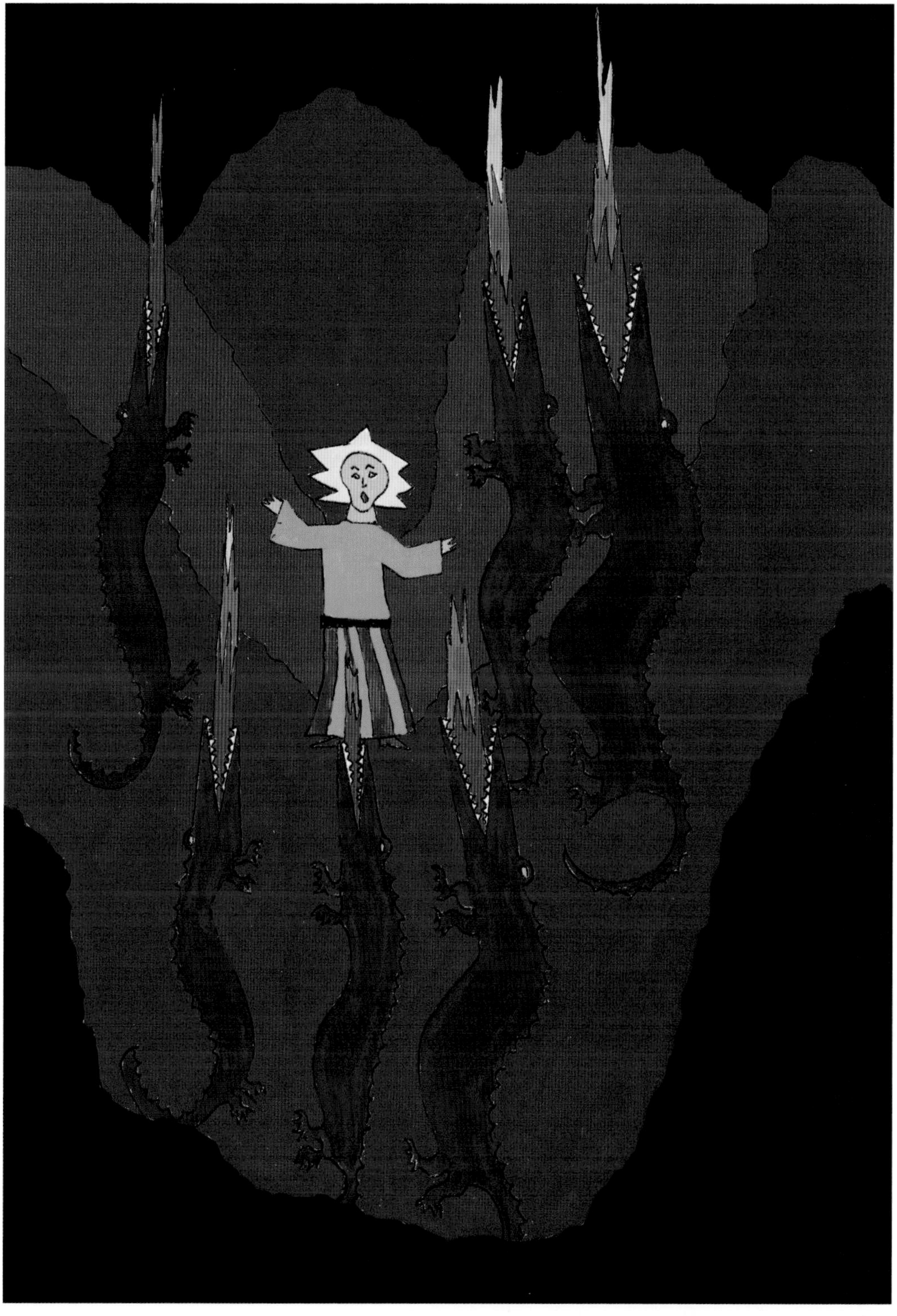

The Kingdom of the Frogs is a subterranean kingdom in the outer reaches of Ramion. Huge man-eating frogs seized Griselda, bound her with strong ropes and attached her to an altar with metal clasps, ready to sacrifice her to the great god Karr.

Once more Sir Tancred appeared beside her, sacrificial sword in one hand, glass of evil spirit in the other. "Drink this you little scum and I will take you back to Grunch Castle! Otherwise I shall sacrifice you to the great god Karr."

Placing sword on the altar stone Sir Tancred bent down, opened Griselda's mouth with finger and thumb and tried to pour the evil spirit down her throat. But Griselda was a girl of spirit. Biting Sir Tancred's fingers hard she spat the evil spirit in his eye and cried, "Sacrifice me. I do not care. I hate you."

Licking bitten fingers Sir Tancred bellowed in anger. How could a five – year – old be so stubborn? (He did not know much about children). He was out of his depth. He needed help. He would seek help from the source of evil. Raising his arm with a magic curse he transported Griselda to the Land of Nothingness.

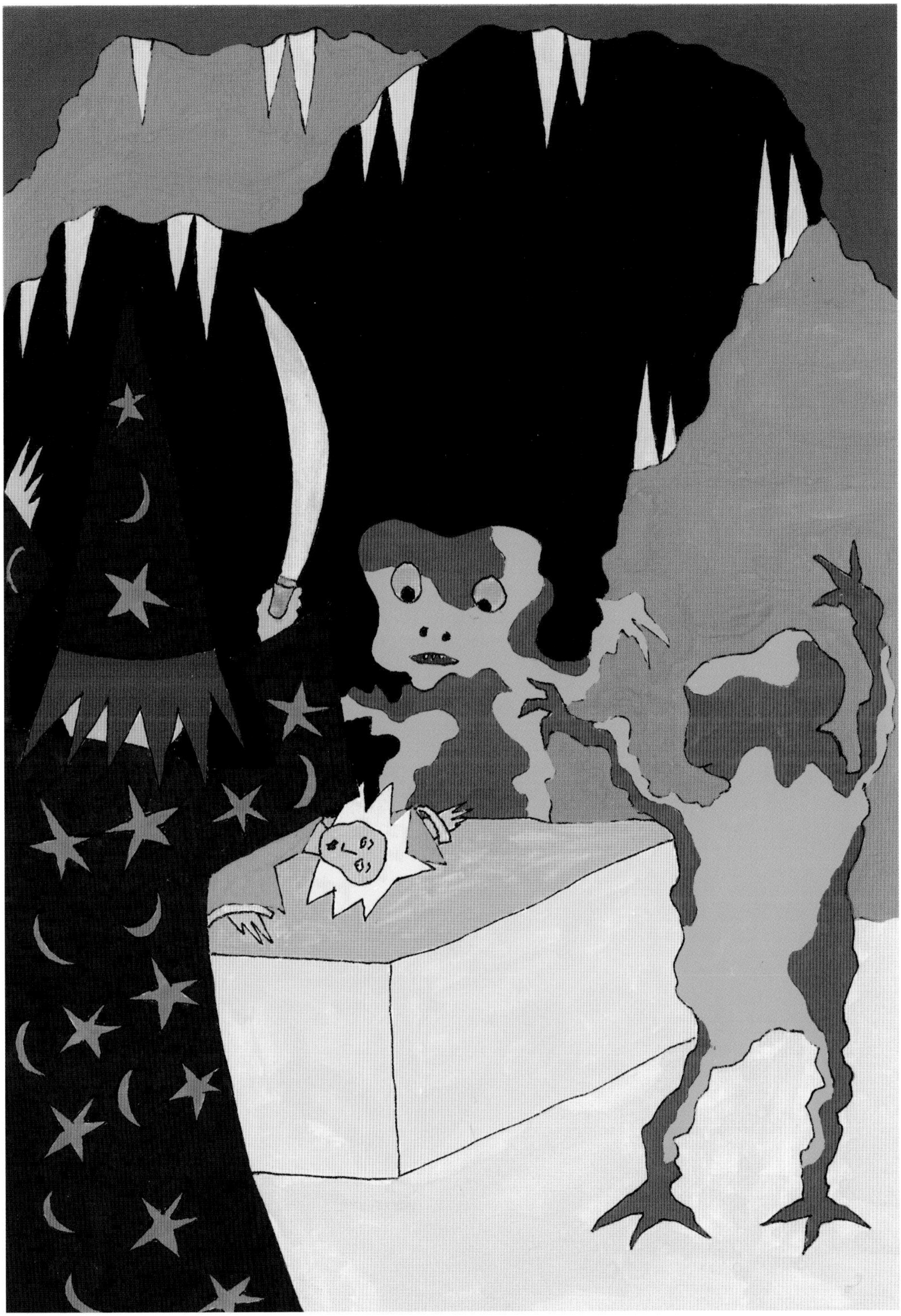

Griselda fell and fell through the void and landed, her limbs changed to nothingness. Even she was a little frightened. In that land nothing had substance, all was mist in different shades of swirling grey. She floated, hardly able to distinguish between different shades of grey, where foot or arm ended and ground or sky began. If she met a tree or rock of solid mist, her body swirled around it. She had not travelled far when out of the mist there rode a princess of swirling shades of black and grey upon a horse of nothingness. Beside her strode Sir Tancred, his body also changed to nothingness.

"Griselda, bow to the Princess of the Night," cried Sir Tancred. "Bow to the source of evil. Bow to the Princess from whom our family derives its power."

"Shall not. She's horrid. Leave me here. I do not care. I hate you."

Sir Tancred turned to the Princess in despair. "You see how stubborn she is. It is completely hopeless. I shall never be able to get her to drink the evil spirit."

The Princess smiled, a horrid smile. She could recognise evil. She knew how to make evil grow. She whispered to Sir Tancred, "You are wrong. I have already sown the seed of evil in her. It will grow. You must forbid her evil spirit."

"Forbid her evil spirit!" hissed Sir Tancred in a whisper. "Your Highness I am sorry, but that is madness. I need an heir. I need a member of the Grunch family to follow the path of evil."

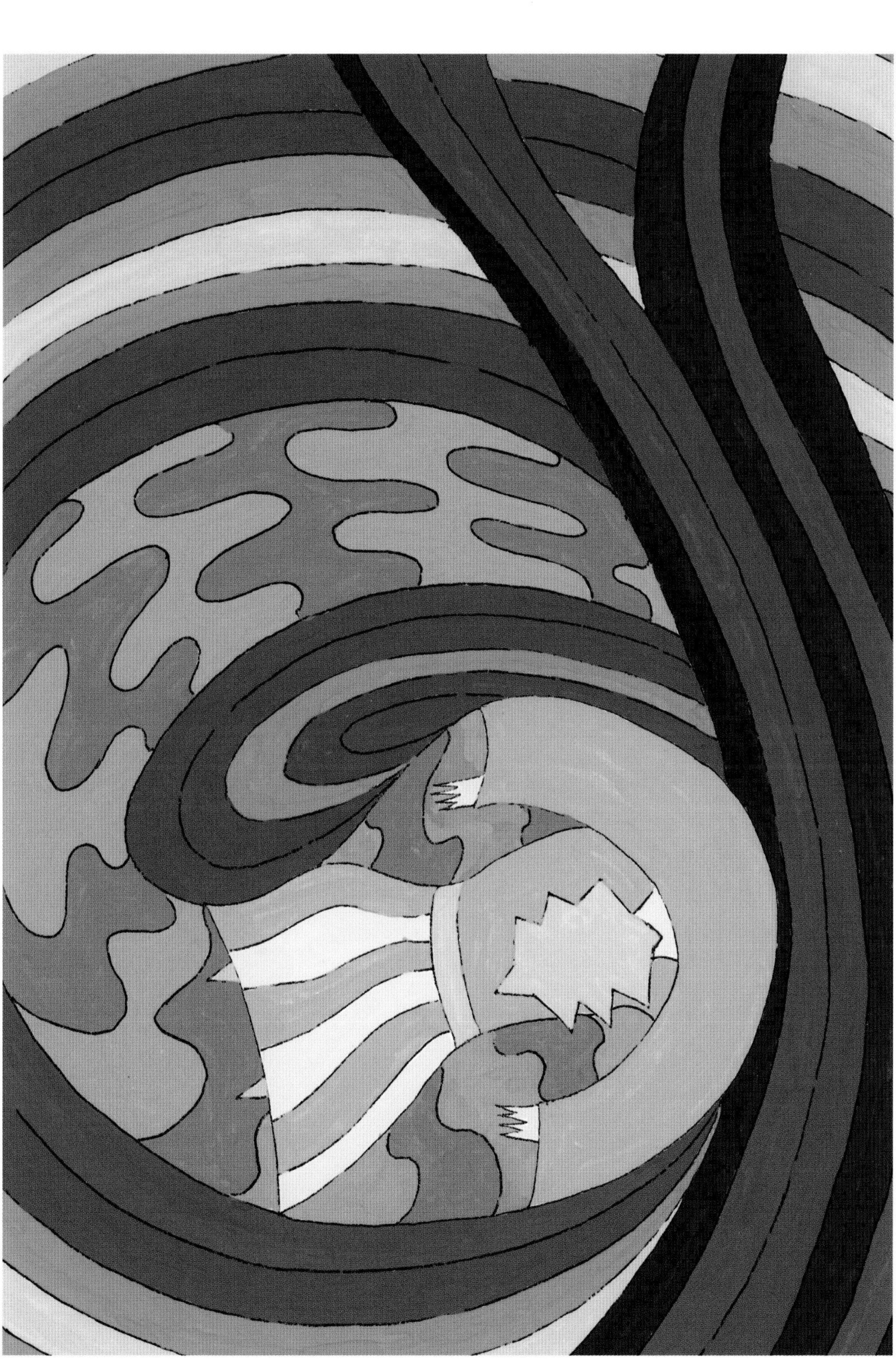

"You will get your heir," the Princess replied. "Griselda will be a worthy successor in the ways of evil. But she is stubborn. Anything you want she will not do. Forbid her to drink the evil spirit, but leave bottles around the castle. One day she will start to drink."

The Princess then turned to Griselda. "You have done well. Your grandfather has put you to a test, to see whether you had the courage to resist, to see whether you are worthy to train as a witch. You have passed. Now go." So saying the Princess raised her magic staff and uttered another spell. Griselda travelled through space and found herself once more in the bedroom in the ruined tower. But this time the door was unlocked and on the table underneath the window a feast of everything she liked to eat and drink.

"Great!" Griselda cried, tucking in. "I am glad I passed the test. I have always wanted to be a witch, ever since 'itch came to me on my first birthday." She began to dream about what it would be like when she grew up and became a proper witch, a traditional witch, not a modern wishy-washy witch, but the sort of witch in the tales of The Sisters Grimm and Hans Lucifer Andersen. "I shall have guards to bow down before me, guards to fatten up captured children, a floating skull to perform my every wish and if he is naughty I shall kick him!" She clapped her hands in glee. "It will be absolutely super!"

Griselda was young and foolish, and did not know that there dwelt within her, as in every human being, the power of love which can conquer all.

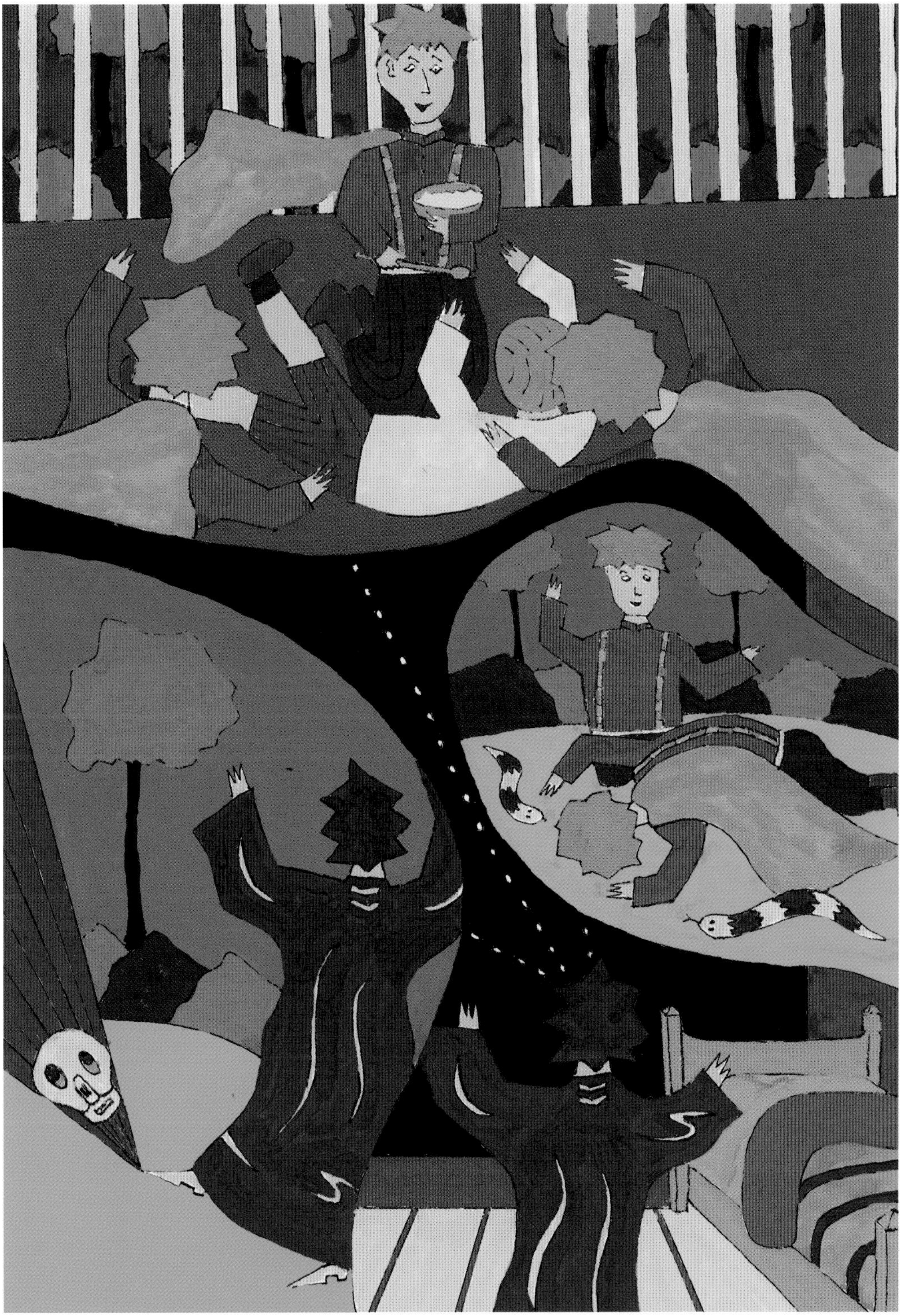

Available Now:

TALES OF RAMION
THE LAND OF LOST HAIR
Frank Hinks

THE LAND OF LOST HAIR

No. 1

When Snuggle takes the boys to the Land of Lost Hair, Griselda follows and sends giant combs, scissors and hair driers to get the boys. "Boy kebabs for tea!" cried Griselda jubilantly.

ISBN: 9781909938106

TALES OF RAMION
THE VICAR'S CHICKENS
Frank Hinks

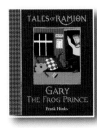

THE VICAR'S CHICKENS

No. 2

When Griselda sends fireballs on the garden of The Old Vicarage, Snuggle by mistake magics not only the boys but the church and Vicar to the Land of Ramion with strange results.

ISBN: 9781909938168

TALES OF RAMION
THE CRYSTAL KEY
Frank Hinks

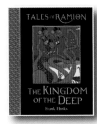

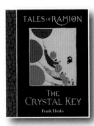

THE CRYSTAL KEY

No. 3

Griselda imprisons Snuggle in a block of crystal, sets the block in hills where the mind controls. Unless the cat can be set free the Gardener will die (and with him the Land of Ramion).

ISBN: 9781909938120

TALES OF RAMION
CREATURES OF THE FOREST
Frank Hinks

CREATURES OF THE FOREST

No. 4

In the forest the boys and Scrooey-Looey brave Globerous Ghosts, Venomous Vampires, Scary Scots and Mystic Mummies, who (like other mummies) cannot stand boys picking their noses.

ISBN: 9781909938144

TALES OF RAMION
GARY
THE FROG PRINCE
Frank Hinks

GARY THE FROG PRINCE

No. 11

When Gary is kissed by the Frog Princess and turned into a Frog Prince, Snuggle takes him, Scrooey-Looey and the boys to the Kingdom of the Frogs where they meet man-eating frogs.

ISBN: 9781909938236

TALES OF RAMION
THE KINGDOM OF THE DEEP
Frank Hinks

THE KINGDOM OF THE DEEP

No. 13

Not allowed by her cousin Veronica to eat the boys whilst in Morgan Castle, Griselda magics them to the Kingdom of the Deep where with octopus, squid and mermen she tries to get them.

ISBN: 9781909938250

TALES OF RAMION
THE BLIZZARD WIZARD
Frank Hinks

THE BLIZZARD WIZARD

No. 14

When with the help of foolish Cloud 9 the Princess of the Night frees the Blizzard Wizard from his prison cell, he turns the Garden, the Gardener and the whole of Ramion into ice.

ISBN: 9781909938274

TALES OF RAMION
THE BODY COLLECTOR
Frank Hinks

THE BODY COLLECTOR

No. 15

Boris the skull will only rescue Griselda from the Mini-skulls if she promises to get back his body, but when Griselda and Boris visit the Body Collector nothing works out as they expect

ISBN: 9781909938205

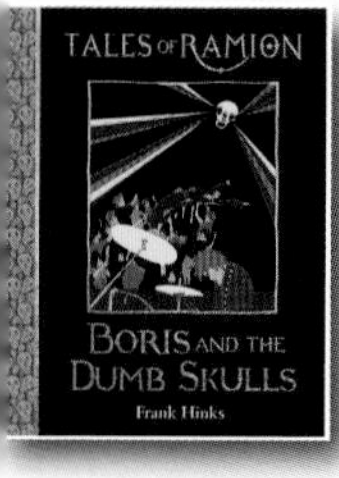
TALES OF RAMION
BORIS AND THE DUMB SKULLS
Frank Hinks

Boris and the Dumb Skulls

No. 16

Boris and the Dim Daft Dwarves form a punk rock band, but just before their first gig Griselda's dead ancestor (Fifi Vicomtesse De Grunch) breaks out of her glass tank and joins the dance.

ISBN: 9781909938182

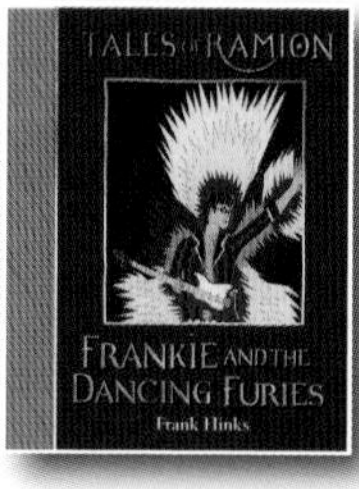
TALES OF RAMION
FRANKIE AND THE DANCING FURIES
Frank Hinks

Frankie and the Dancing Furies No. 18

A storm summoned by Griselda carries off the boys' father (along with others) to the Land of the Dancing Furies where the spirit of the rock god Jimi (Hendrix) takes possession of his body

ISBN: 9781909938083

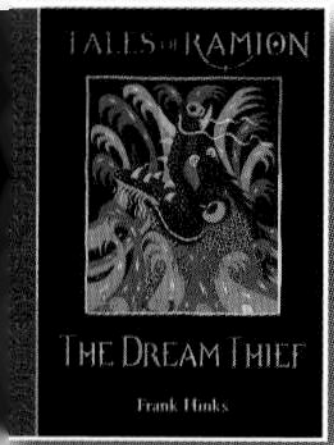
TALES OF RAMION
THE DREAM THIEF
Frank Hinks

The Dream Thief

No. 17

When the Dream Thief steals their mother's dream the boys and Snuggle travel to rescue it, braving fish with fishing rods, butterflies with butterfly nets, and game birds bearing shotguns.

ISBN: 9781909938021

TALES OF RAMION

You can explore the magical world of Ramion by visiting the website

www.ramion-books.com

Share Ramion Moments on Facebook

TALES of RAMION
FACT AND FANTASY

O nce upon a time not so long ago there lived in The Old Vicarage, Shoreham, Kent (a village south of London) three boys (Julius, Alexander and Benjamin) with their mother, father and Snuggle, the misnamed family cat who savaged dogs and had a weakness for the vicar's chickens. At birthdays there were magic shows with Scrooey-Looey, a glove puppet with great red mouth who was always rude.

The boys with Snuggle

J ulius was a demanding child. Each night he wanted a different story. But he would help his father. "Dad tonight I want a story about the witch Griselda" (who had purple hair like his artist mother) "and the rabbit Scrooey-Looey and it starts like this…" His father then had to take over the story not knowing where it was going (save that the witch was not allowed to eat the children). Out of such stories grew the Tales of Ramion which were enacted with the boys' mother as Griselda and the boys' friends as Griselda's guards, the Dim Daft Dwarves (a role which came naturally to children).

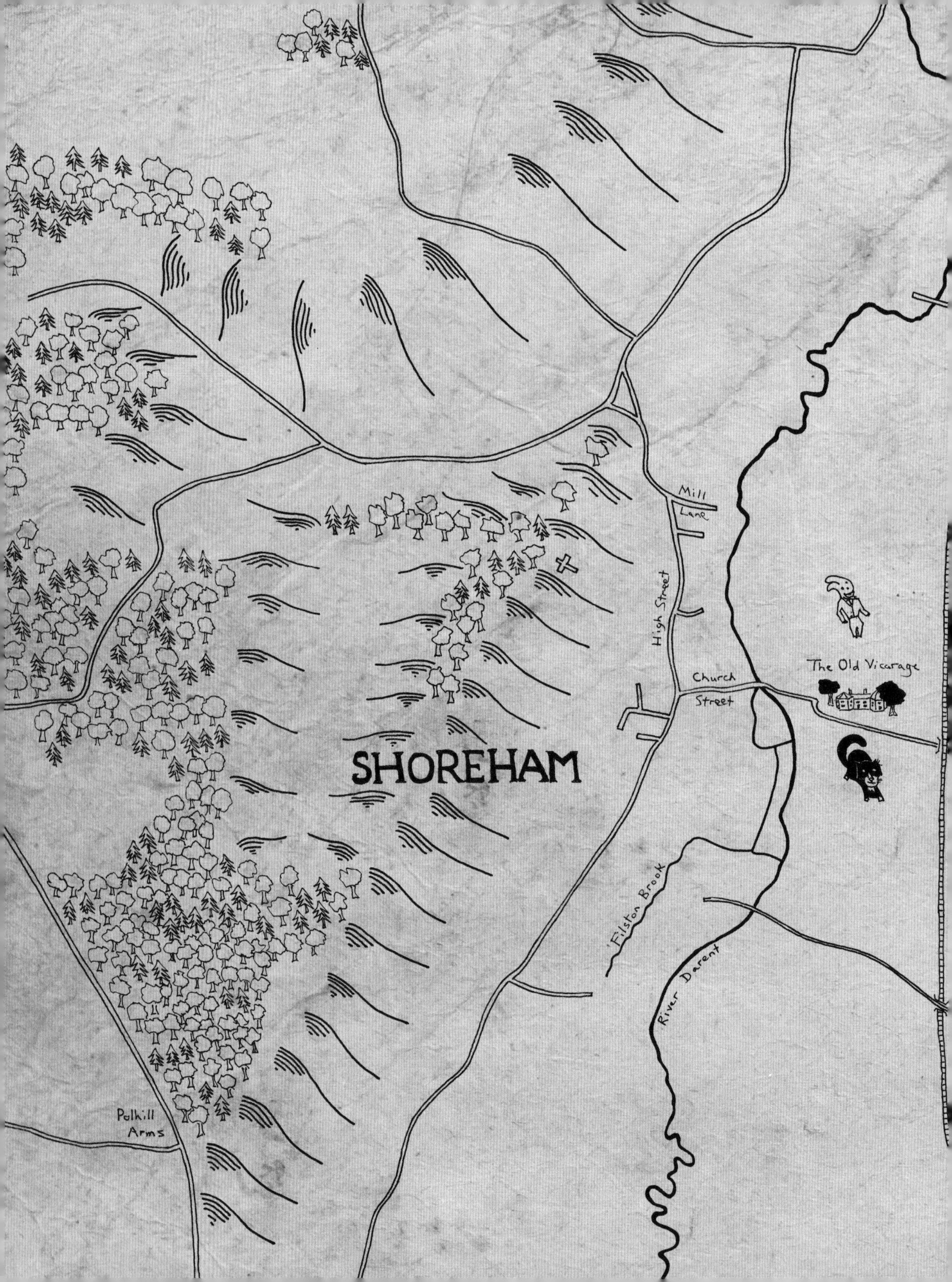
SHOREHAM
Mill Lane
High Street
Church Street
The Old Vicarage
Filston Brook
River Darent
Polhill Arms